FROM WATSON'S SCRAPBOOK

Holmes is actually looking forward to our next issue, for in terms of ego, which he possesses in abundance, the fifteenth edition of *Sherlock Holmes Mystery Magazine* will be devoted entirely to our detectival adventures, one of which, though a slight little thing of my authorship, will be unfamiliar to many readers. In addition, there will be some ten new stories prepared by various scribes from my original notes.

Two stories are, I think, of especial interest. The first, prepared by a New York scribe named Eugene D. Goodwin, tells of a case that Holmes undertook on behalf of that eccentric genius Nikola Tesla—an investigation that led my friend to cross paths again with that Napoleon of Crime—well, you know who I mean.

One might think that Tesla must be our most unusual client, but not quite, for the second adventure to which I have referred and which was prepared by Ms Carole Buggé (also known as C E Lawrence) actually brings Holmes and me face to face with a sinister client to whom I have just alluded.

Now in this issue, in addition to my own recounting of that problem I call "A Case of Identity" is "The Adventure of the Empty Lighthouse," another Holmesian tale, this time rendered from my notes by that excellent Pennsylvania scribe Jack Grochot. And to my amazement and delight, Michael Mallory has written up a case that involved neither Holmes nor me, but none other than Mrs Hudson!

And now I shall turn you over to my colleague, Mr Kaye.

—John H. Watson, M. D.

✗　✗　✗　✗

I, too, am eagerly looking forward to our upcoming all-Holmes issue, the third such since *Sherlock Holmes Mystery Magazine* got under way in 2008. But this does not mean that the present issue was sloughed off; it contains, in addition to the three Holmes stories, no fewer than eleven tales of crime and skullduggery from (alphabetically) newcomer Jason Barnhart, Gerald Elias, Mary Laufer, BV Lawson, Laird Long, Meg Opperman, Stan Trybulski, Kelli A. Wilkins, and George Zebrowski.

Yes, that's only nine stories. I reserve special praise for a new story by John M. Floyd about "Sheriff Lucy Valentine and her crimefighting mother Fran." These two sometimes-bickering ladies have appeared several times already in the pages of this magazine, and they are always welcome to return!

—Canonically yours,
Marvin Kaye

SHERLOCK HOLMES
MYSTERY MAGAZINE

#14 (VOLUME 5 NUMBER 4)   July/August 2014

Publisher: John Betancourt
Editor: Marvin Kaye
Assistant Editors: Steve Coupe, Sam Cooper

Sherlock Holmes Mystery Magazine is published by Wildside Press, LLC. Single copies: $10.00 + $3.00 postage. U.S. subscriptions: $59.95 (postage paid) for the next 6 issues in the U.S.A., from: Wildside Press LLC, Subscription Dept. 9710 Traville Gateway Dr., #234; Rockville MD 20850. International subscriptions: see our web site at www.wildsidemagazines.com. Available as an ebook through all major ebook etailers, or our web site, www.wildsidemagazines.com.

COMING NEXT TIME...

**STORIES! ARTICLES!
SHERLOCK HOLMES & DR. WATSON!**

Sherlock Holmes Mystery Magazine #15
is just a few months away...watch for it!

REVIEW: DOYLE AFTER DEATH, BY JOHN SHIRLEY

by Kim Newman

A murder mystery set in the afterlife, this teams the long-established shade of Arthur Conan Doyle, creator of the Great Detective, with Nicholas Fogg, a just-dead Las Vegas PI with a burden of guilts carried over from life. In the world of Shirley's novel, the land beyond death is different but still physical, and even the departed can be dispelled. Wittily, we are told that Philip José Farmer passed through here looking for the aliens he believed were responsible, since this small-town universe owes quite a bit to his visions of resurrection on *Riverworld* and perhaps also to Arthur Byron Cover's *An East Wind Coming*.

As a whodunit, this has the feel of a 1970s TV movie—it's guessable at a stretch, but the suspects are all pleasant company and the working-out of the crime is interesting. It's a convenience that the departed mellow somewhat, so Doyle doesn't seem too upset to learn that this isn't the plane he was expecting when he embraced spiritualism—or that his son Kingsley has told him that none of the spirit messages he received through mediums in life were really from him. Shirley fills in more about the world in a series of chatty appendixes, but doesn't take any great philosophical position on where we go—the quiet resort of Garden Rest is a way station, like the ones in the play *Outward Bound* or the movie *Haunts of the Very Rich*, not a Heaven or Hell.

Fogg, who narrates, has a noirish sensibility, which contrasts with Doyle's still-burning Edwardian idealism—but it takes both to crack the case. In an impressive set-piece, the pair venture into a collapsing mansion, or rather an idea of a mansion where the process of imaginative creation necessary to build anything in the afterlife has metastasized to surreal effect. A brisk, readable, smart novel, this has the feel of the beginning of a series—I'd certainly like to see more of Doyle and Fogg and the dead folks who pass through Garden Rest.

✗

REVIEW: HYDE, BY DANIEL LEVINE

by Kim Newman

For a book which displaces an enormous amount of cultural water, Robert Louis Stevenson's *Strange Case of Dr Jekyll andMr Hyde* (1886) is remarkably slim. It is reprinted in its entirety as a ninety-page addendum to Daniel Levine's *Hyde*—a useful strategy which allows the reader to see how closely the new novelist has stuck to Stevenson's surprisingly intricate plotting, even as he plays the now-familiar game (cf: *Wide Sargasso Sea*, *The Dracula Tape*, *Phantom*, *Wicked*) of telling a well-known story from the viewpoint, suppressed in the original, of the 'monster'. This usually requires a certain amount of setting-aside of matters established in the original text. Here, after Dr Jekyll has written his statement of the case (the concluding and revelatory chapter of Stevenson's novel), his alter ego sits down and writes a counter-version, promising to be truthful where Jekyll is evasive. *Hyde* elaborates on a few things Stevenson mentions or implies but doesn't explore (Hyde's domestic arrangements in Soho), delves deeper (arguably) into the split (now, multiple) personality of the protagonist (there's a third shard in the mix, Hyde's own Hyde, inevitably tagged Mr Seek), more firmly roots the story in the era in which it was written by linking Hyde's vices with those exposed by the editor W.T. Stead in his 'Maiden Tribute of Modern Babylon' campaign in the *Pall Mall Gazette* and explores Jekyll's unhappy childhood and involvement with the beginnings of psychiatry.

Like stage/film adaptations of the story all the way back to the 1880s, *Hyde* makes up significant new characters, introducing contrasted women (Dr Jekyll's fragile ex-girlfriend, Mr Hyde's underage mistress) to represent the strata of society inhabited by the good doctor and the bad mister. Unlike many takes on the story, the women are not so prominent as to distract from the fact that this tale is all about a man's relationship with himself. Indeed, Jekyll's ex, Georgiana, and his kept woman, Jeannie, are less intriguing than Mrs Deaker, the housekeeper Stevenson mentions but doesn't name, who is Hyde's disapproving enabler and turns out to be a more complicated and sinister presence. This material has been worked over before, of course. Indeed, almost every adaptation of the Stevenson story (stage, film, radio, comics, TV) has added, elaborated or revised the original work (not least because it has a twist ending everyone knows). Several other novels have spun off from the *Strange Case*. The most notable literary revision of Jekyll and Hyde is Valerie Martin's *Mary Reilly*, but Chuck Pahlaniuk's *Fight Club* is also—upon close examination—a contemporary re-think of Stevenson's premise and theme. *Hyde* isn't quite as strong as *Mary Reilly*, which was written before there were enough of these things around (one of the jacket quotes on *Hyde* is from Ronald Frame, author of *Havisham*) to establish conventions for the sub-genre.

A primary requirement of these revisitings, dating back to George Macdonald Fraser's *Flashman* books is that outright villains prove more reliable narrators than their righteous foes. There's a sly arrogance as contemporary writers set out to 'correct' classic authors whose works have lasted long enough to make re-visitings of their creations a commercially worthwhile enterprise. It also amounts to special pleading on the part of characters whose dastardliness has always been a given. Levine's Hyde retells the incident of the trampled child so that the waif is a calculating aggressor and her family eager to extort payment from a passing toff. It's well-enough handled, but the scene pales beside Stevenson's original master-stroke that the ultimate evil is also a terrified, pathetic *little* man. A complicated relationship is established between Jekyll (and Hyde) and Sir Danvers Carew, the Member of Parliament Hyde bludgeons to death with Jekyll's cane, suggesting a calculating Jekyll exploiting the vicious Hyde. All the historical research and a grounding in the way Jekyll has been warped by his own upbringing marks this out as a serious book, which regrettably means it has to claw back Stevenson's more fantastical 'fine bogey tale'. Levine's Jekyll takes his addictive potion by injection, though it's almost a placebo—the person who comes to be called Hyde already exists. Jekyll adopts a different posture and expression (and wears his father's oversized clothes), but doesn't actually undergo the type of metamorphosis described in Stevenson and used as a set-piece in most film versions. This isn't a particularly unusual approach—Anthony Perkins (in *Edge of Sanity*, 1989) and

John Hannah (in *Dr Jekyll and Mr Hyde*, 2003) play Jekyll and Hyde in essentially this manner.

Levine works hard on making his Victorian London a physical environment (though he oddly and jarringly uses American forms when giving street addresses) but also filtering the world through the sensibility of Hyde, who has an eye for repellent detail. The book still needs a monster, so Mr Seek—who takes over when Hyde has blackouts—is vaguely present throughout, sometimes intruding with childish notes and mantras. It does engage with the Stevenson in a gripping, sometimes startling manner, but there's a slight sense of coming late to the party. When the actor-manager Richard Mansfield hired the playwright T. Russell Sullivan to turn the novella into a stage drama in 1887, he began the process of taking Jekyll and Hyde away from Stevenson and disseminating the story throughout the culture…where it is a vital, evolving presence in everything from *The Nutty Professor* to *The Incredible Hulk*. *Hyde* is an interesting addition to the shelf of Jekyll and Hyde spin-offs, but it's unlikely to be the last word.

REVIEW: SHERLOCK HOLMES AND THE GHOSTS OF BLY, BY DONALD THOMAS

by Kim Newman

The English historian, biographer, and novelist Donald Thomas has crafted several volumes of Sherlockian pastiche, starting with *The Secret Cases of Sherlock Holmes* (1997) and extending to *Death on a Pale Horse: Sherlock Holmes on Her Majesty's Secret Service* (2013). Thomas sticks close to the Doyle model in employing Dr Watson as narrator, making occasional references to canonical stories and presenting Holmes as a rational sleuth even when tackling cases that seem to involve the supernatural. Thomas has become comfortable with his own versions of Holmes and Watson and found voices for them which are recognisable as the established characters but also have eccentricities and enthusiasms peculiar to his own work.

This collection features three cases (and one biographical essay which sets up the third case but is oddly presented as a separate chapter) which find Holmes in varied well-researched milieux. The title story is a double pastiche, tipping Doyle's characters into another writer's story; the other cases are an *a clef* elaboration on an actual historical crime remembered for its earlier fictionalisation and a mystery that, refreshingly, comes from whole cloth and is perhaps the most satisfying in the set.

'The Case of a Boy's Honour' finds Holmes and Watson still in Baker Street in 1913 (though Holmes's retirement is mentioned elsewhere in the book) and retained by Admiral Sir John Fisher to represent Cadet Patrick Riley, a lad accused of stealing a postal order at a Naval Academy. It's a peculiarity of Thomas's Holmes that he is hired by or commissioned to represent the interests of clients accused or even convicted of crimes ranging from pilfering (and forgery) to murder…this slightly varies from Doyle's detective, whose interest tended to be piqued by the puzzle rather than a cause. This incident would seem to be beneath the abilities of the premier sleuth of the age (Thomas's Holmes also trades on his reputation) but, of course, the historical incident behind the mystery also became a national sensation. Terence Rattigan's play *The Winslow Boy* was based on a trial which involved a cadet called George Archer-Shee. Thomas sticks a little closer to the story than Rattigan, setting the academy (a crammer for Naval college, not a Navy-approved institution) on the Isle of White where Archer-Shee's alleged crime took place. He adds a seeming suicide attempt on the railway tracks that leads to a paraphrase of a famous speech from *Double Indemnity*, a reason for Fisher to be involved since a clash of hidebound tradition and forward-thinking innovation is a major motivation in the villains's misdeeds and several other sub-plots (Thomas's cases generally run twice the length of Doyle's, sometimes considerably longer). It's an interesting bit of speculation and historical embroidery on a well-known case—*The Winslow Boy* is all about exonerating its stubborn schoolboy, but this delves into the reasons why he might have been framed. Still, even with the issues at stake, Holmes is rather too big a gun to be fired off here…the final battle of wits is not with a mature mastermind worth his mettle, but a teenage bully who cracks as soon as the game is rumbled. Fisher, featured in earlier Thomas Holmes stories, is an interesting historical character responsible for a) the modernisation of the Royal Navy in the years before World War I and b) coining the currently-popular textspeak term OMG.

'The Case of the Ghost at Bly' is novel-length and a sequel to Henry James's *The Turn of the Screw*. Holmes is hired to get Victoria Temple—James's unnamed governess—released from Broadmoor Asylum by proving that she was not instrumental in the deaths of her young charges and that the hauntings at Bly have an entirely natural explanation. This also exposes a series of earthly crimes including the murder of Peter Quint, whose spectre is supposed to have driven Miss Temple mad. It's well-argued, in that it takes the account given in James's novel—itself bracketed by a 'discovered manuscript' device and a club-room debate about ghost stories which renders the governess a questionable narrator—and plays scrupulously fair with each described transgression of the supernatural on the mortal plane while having Holmes winkle out an alternative explanation. Of course, James was a master of ambiguity and the point of this brand of mystery is to shine light into darkness and clear up all the mysteries…which means that there's a slight sense of disappointment in the solution. Also, as the longest piece in the book, it hares off once its dastardly villain has been exposed and turns into a chase sequence that merely delays the inevitable. An aside about spiritualism seems to dangle, opening up a can of worms the devout spiritualist Doyle knew better than to take off the shelf.

'Sherlock Holmes the Actor' elaborates on W.S. Baring-Gould's notion of Holmes's spell on the stage perfecting his mastery of disguise, but basically sets up the career of Sir Henry Caradoc Price, a Welsh tragedian and rival to Henry Irving whose murder—apparently poisoned onstage while playing Claudius—is the plot motor of 'The Case of the Matinee Idol'. Thomas enjoys Price, who is an unredeemed wrecker of careers and despoiler of young ladies surrounded by people with motives to do him ill and the theatreland of the story is vivid and credible. Without any particular historical or literary axe to grind, this is perhaps the most purely entertaining piece in the book...a loathesome swine is dead, a scarcely more likeable fellow is accused and the police are intent on running down a blind alley while Holmes works tenaciously at the puzzle (cigar ash comes into it) and then sees that justice is served if not done.

ASK MRS HUDSON

by Mrs Martha Hudson

This issue I only have one letter to share with you. It is quite an old one, but it resulted in a truly unusual situation that I finally feel able to tell you about.

Here is the letter:

⚔ ⚔ ⚔ ⚔

To the capitalist landlady of Messrs Holmes and Watson,

You probably do not know who I am, though I imagine that your tenants might, or at least Mr Holmes. Certainly I am aware of both of these gentlemen, for I have long admired their exploits. I particularly value Mr Holmes for often not accepting fees.

Now to my problem. I have considered consulting with Dr Watson, but I think it prudent to solicit your opinion before taking action that might precipitate some danger at 221 Baker Street.

You see, there are a number of dissidents from my mother-land who wish me dead and have every intention of making it happen. They have pursued me across Asia and Europe and though for the moment I have eluded them, I am sure that they will track me down.

I have devised a plan to prevent my assassination. It requires medical assistance. I am sure that Dr Watson is a man of unimpeachable morals and discretion. But because of the potential danger to which I have alluded, I feel it wise to ask your advice first.

The messenger who delivers this to you is utterly trustworthy. Kindly send your reply to me through him.

—Karl Marx

⚔ ⚔ ⚔ ⚔

I told his messenger that I could not write an answer until I spoke with Dr Watson, who was engaged at that time treating patients at his office in another part of London. The man nodded and said he would return the following day.

Mr Holmes was puttering about in his laboratory and I almost showed him the letter, but then I decided that I should respect Mr Marx's wishes and deal with the doctor, at least at first. Well, by the time the messenger returned the following afternoon, I had spoken with both of my tenants and, as a result, wrote this reply:

✗ ✗ ✗

My Dear Mr Marx,

Dr Watson is willing to meet with you. He suggests that you seek him out at his medical office at the junction of Solar Square and Praed Street.

—Mrs Hudson

✗ ✗ ✗ ✗

He did just that, and the outcome is what I perhaps fancifully call "The Case of the Dead Revolutionary."

Dr Watson later told me (this was in Mr Holmes's presence) that when Mr Marx appeared at his office, he (the doctor) discovered that the man was a Russian who had been living for a time in London. "He has written a tract about this new governmental philosophy called Communism. You may know about a similar, but much gentler movement that has been talked about here in Britain. I am referring to what has been labeled Socialism."

Well, I shall not bore you with the details of a political movement that I am sure soon will be all but forgotten. Let me continue, instead, with Dr Watson's tale.

"It is a good thing that you referred him to me," he said, "and it was also prudent to send him to my practice, rather than Baker Street."

"So what is he like?" I asked.

He scowled. "He is a dreadful rascal. Brilliant, perhaps, but totally without charm and, I suspect, ruthless. It is ironic that he is worried about assassination, for I am sure he is not only capable of murder, but quite likely has already done the deed."

"What does he look like, Doctor?"

"He affects a rough, unkept appearance. A bit stocky and with so much hair one can hardly see any of his face except for his eyes, which suggested to me that the man is utterly mad."

Up till now, Mr Holmes had said nothing, but now he spoke up. "What advice did you give him, Watson?"

"Oh, Holmes, at first I had no idea how to sidestep dealing with him, so for a time, I allowed him to do all of the talking. He outlined his efforts to escape his pursuers, and described what he thought they'd do to him if they managed to capture him." He glanced at me. "I will spare you the details, Mrs Hudson."

"What is the plan he alluded to in his letter?" Holmes asked.

"He wishes to have it announced that he is dead."

His friend shook his head. "They—his enemies—won't believe that."

"No, Holmes, he not only plans to announce it, he means to have an actual funeral with himself on view in an open coffin."

I laughed mirthlessly. "And I suppose he plans to stop breathing?"

"He told me that he has mastered the ability to breathe so shallowly as to be virtually undetectable. He demonstrated and it was quite convincing."

"Perhaps that is true," I said, "but what about his *pulse*?!"

"He is actually able to stop it at will. He showed me that, too, and I swear to you, Mrs Hudson, that he had no pulse at all!"

It was too much for me but then Mr Holmes nodded his head. "It's an old circus trick. I can do it, too…or could if I had the equipment. Tell me, Watson, when he stopped his pulse, did you take note of his physical stance?"

"He was standing casually. No, wait! His left arm—"

"Yes?" Holmes prompted.

"It looked like this." The doctor pressed it tightly against his side.

"Then he is using the very secret I have mentioned."

Both of us wanted details, of course, but sometimes Mr Holmes has a maddening flair for the dramatic. "I'll tell you both later."

"How much later, Holmes?!"

"Has Mr Marx set the date for his funeral?"

A decisive nod. "The day after tomorrow."

"Then that's when I will tell you." And with that, Sherlock Holmes retired to his room, where we soon heard him playing the violin.

"Mrs Hudson," the good doctor said, "I do believe that if we poisoned his tea, we would be acquitted."

"I agree," I said with a smile. "It would be justifiable homicide."

Two days later, we all dressed up in dark clothing and went to Mr Marx's funeral. It was quite well attended. We did not approach the coffin, though we did stand near enough to observe the mourners *y clept* as they took their turns visiting the corpse (who did indeed seem quite deceased, at least to my untrained eyes).

There were ever so many ruffians present and one of them, surreptitiously, but certainly observable by me, Mr Holmes, and Dr Watson, produced a small cosmetics mirror and held it under the dead man's nostrils.

That rattled me, but worse was to come. Another of these villains actually pinched Marx's cheek, tweaked his nose and then tried it again, but at last shrugged and retreated. I thought nothing worse could happen, but the next man actually stuck a needle into Marx's hand!

The corpse just lay there ever so convincingly.

At last I approached the coffin. Mr Marx was as Dr Watson described. He sported a great deal of unruly hair, including a huge moustache and beard. Without doubt, I had to accept that he was indeed in another world.

"Oh, Mr Marx," I said in a low voice, "I regret that we did not meet, and I only look upon your mortal relict. I am that Mrs Hudson you wrote to some days ago."

As I finished speaking to him, one of his eyes opened and the rascal winked at me!

That night, there was a knock at the front door. I opened it and saw a stocky man who was altogether clean-shaven. "Yes?" I asked.

He grinned. "Why, Mrs Hudson, don't you recognize me? I'm Karl Marx."

I was completely flummoxed and partly because I was in my night-gown. "I'm afraid Mr Holmes and Dr Watson have already turned in."

"That's all right. Do thank them for me, though. Here is a present I brought for you." He handed me a gift-wrapped package and then said good-bye.

His gift was a copy of a book he'd written called *The Communist Manifesto*. I tried to read it but it bored me silly.

✗   ✗   ✗   ✗

I have room for one recipe. It is a truly unusual dessert, its origin is Mexico. Although the original calls for using a calabaza gourd and piloncillo, that is, Mexican sugar pillars, these are difficult to find, even in London, so I have substituted much more accessible ingredients: pumpkin and brown sugar.

✗   ✗   ✗   ✗

PUMPKIN IN BROWN SUGAR

1 medium-size pumpkin
Dark brown sugar, one cup for every cup of diced pumpkin
4 orange rinds
4 ounces of cinnamon (see note below)
1 ounce of lime water (see note below)
1 juice glass of light or dark rum, as preferred

Re the cinnamon—the original recipe calls for cinnamon sticks, but these then must be picked out of the cooked pumpkin, so I suggest powdered cinnamon, instead.

Re lime water—this is obtainable from an apothecary/pharmacist.

1. Cut a plug in the pumpkin top and pour in the rum. Replace the plug and let it stand overnight.

2. Early the next day, cut the *unpeeled* pumpkin into squares that are neither too large nor too fat. Throw away the seeds.

3. Place the pumpkin squares in a large bowl and cover with cold water. Add the lime water and let it rest there for one hour, then pour away the water.

4. In a large pot, place one cup of pumpkin squares, then add one cup of brown sugar. Add the cinnamon and orange rind, cut into pieces.

5. Continue this process until all of the pumpkin has been put into the pot.

6. Boil on a mild heat until the pumpkin is quite tender and the resultant syrup has texture. This will take many hours, depending on the size of the pumpkin.

7. Remove from the flames and allow the mixture to cool.

8. Serve it in deep bowls with sweet cream. If preferred, soft cheese may be substituted, or vanilla ice cream.

Do note that you will have a great amount of this dessert on hand. You will need to store it all in covered jars in your ice box.

✗

SLEUTHING: YESTERDAY, TODAY, AND TOMORROW

by Jacqueline Seewald

The mystery novel features a detective or several detectives who investigate a crime or series of crimes. The amateur sleuths can work in any number of unique and unusual professions which provide interesting background and setting for the story. They can live in any place in the world. They can be nosy spinsters who live in small English villages or gifted professors who investigate bizarre historical crimes. From cozy to thriller, the amateur sleuth fascinates readers.

The private detective novel is a mystery genre unto itself. In 1887, Sir Arthur Conan Doyle created Sherlock Holmes, the most famous of all fictional detectives. Sherlock Holmes was not the first fictional detective. However, his name is one we think of immediately. Conan Doyle stated that the character of Holmes was inspired by Dr. Joseph Bell, for whom Doyle had worked as a clerk at the Edinburgh Royal Infirmary. Like Holmes, Bell was noted for drawing large conclusions from small observations. The quirky Holmes was renowned for his insights based on skillful use of observation, deduction, and forensics to solve puzzling cases. Conan Doyle wrote four novels and fifty-six short stories featuring Holmes, and all but four stories are narrated by Holmes's friend, assistant, and biographer, Dr. John Watson. The Sherlock Holmes mystique is still celebrated today in books, short stories, films, and television programs. Holmes, the "consulting detective," still fascinates a modern audience of devotees.

The Golden Age of Detective Fiction, the 1920's and 30's, brought many writers of detective stories to the forefront. British female authors like Agatha Christie are particularly memorable. Of the four "Queens of Crime" of that era: Christie, Dorothy Sayers, Ngaio Marsh, and Margery Allingham, all were English except for Marsh who was a New Zealander.

In the 1930's, the hard-boiled private eye novels began to evolve with American writers. Over the years, many interesting writers have emerged in this genre. Dashiell Hammett, Raymond Chandler, Mickey Spillane, Ross Macdonald, and Robert Parker are just a few of the writers who still resonate with readers. P.I. detectives are tough guys dealing with seedy characters on the mean city streets, the so-called underbelly of society. They are professional detectives who live by a code of honor but rarely earn much for their efforts. They generally have antagonistic relationships with the police and, like the amateur detective, tend to be more intelligent than their professional law enforcement counterparts. The P.I. novel was male-dominated until the late 1970's and early 80's when writers such as Sara Paretsky, Marcia Miller, and Sue Grafton began creating women investigators who were as tough as men. These novels offered more in-depth characterization and, in the case of Paretsky, a social agenda.

The police procedural provides the reader with a different type of detective story. In reality, most crimes are investigated by police. This type of mystery stresses step-by-step procedures followed by professional detectives such as processing crime scenes to collect physical evidence, canvassing the area for witnesses or suspects, postmortem examination of bodies in the case of murders, identifying a victim if that is not known, and interviewing known friends, co-workers, relatives, and associates. The list is often long and tedious. Not generally so in a novel. Although it is agreed that the police procedural should be accurate in portraying what law enforcement officers actually do, it is not necessary to bore readers to death. Like the P.I. novel, this is action-oriented genre fiction. While the plot may be the backbone of a police procedural as O'Neil De Noux, a longtime police officer and homicide detective, observed in an article written for *The Writer* ("How to Write the Police Procedural Novel," October 1992 issue), the novel won't interest readers unless there are well-developed central characters. Distinctive places also add interest to the modern police procedural. For example, moody Scandinavian settings have provided bleak backgrounds for the investigations of Inspector Martin Beck (Sjöwall and Wahlöö in the 1960's) or Wallander (Henning Mankell) and more recently Inspector Tell (Camilla Cedar).

It goes without saying that all books should be researched for accuracy of detail. However, Eric Wright observes (*The Writer*, October 1990 issue, p. 9) that writers should do their research last. His reasoning: once a story is written the writer will know what information is actually needed and necessary. Collecting unnecessary facts proves to be a waste of valuable time. I am of the opinion that it also leads to information dumping as many writers then cannot resist the temptation to include material that should be cut and which has no purpose in the book or story.

Of course, the more traditional view is that authors who write police procedurals must insist on total accuracy. Margaret Maron, for instance, has explained how she used interviews with police detectives and civil service clerks, attended "criminalistics" classes and took notes on the trivia associated with everyday police activities in a station house to depict realism in her police novel series (*The Writer*, June 1993 issue).

Patricia D. Cornwell's novels have long graced the bestseller lists. Her Dr. Kay Scarpetta forensic pathologist crime novels are strongly associated with her own career. Cornwell describes herself as having been a crime reporter. The character of Dr. Scarpetta appears to have been initially inspired by an interview she had with a female medical examiner. She went to work for the medical examiners and eventually became their computer analyst. Her opinion: stories that lack credibility and authenticity will be unread (*The Writer*, December 1991, pp. 18-20). P. D. James is another author of police procedurals we can describe as the real deal. James held a position as a senior employee in the Criminal Policy Department in England. Joseph Wambaugh has given us some memorable characters who happen to be police officers based on his personal experience and knowledge.

Although I have never written a P.I. novel, my Kim Reynolds mystery series includes both an amateur sleuth as the main character plus police detectives. The main focus of the series, however, has always been on Kim who is an academic librarian, a reluctant sleuth, and a repressed psychic. In *The Inferno Collection*, Kim is contacted at her university library by a friend who believes she is being targeted for murder. When Lorette Campbell dies under mysterious circumstances, Kim tries to convince the police that her friend has not committed suicide as they believe but was in fact murdered. This begins her association with police lieutenant Mike Gardner. In the second book in this series, *The Drowning Pool*, murders occur in Kim's garden apartment complex. Mike, his new partner, African-American policewoman Bert St. Croix, and Kim work in tandem to discover the murderer. In *The Truth Sleuth*, murders occur at the local high school. All three main characters are involved in discovering the identity of the killer. In the latest book in the series, *The Bad Wife*, Mike is accused of murder and it is up to Kim and Bert to help him by discovering the real culprit. Although these books have some elements of both the amateur sleuth and police procedural, they are in fact cross-genre mystery fiction combining elements of romance, the paranormal, and suspense with mystery. This I believe is becoming more of a trend in modern mystery fiction. The traditional lines are blurring and authors are experimenting with a greater variety of style and technique in a genre that is now more dynamic, fluid, and exciting. What stays the same is the need for a well-developed plot, well-rounded and well-defined characters, and a distinctive setting.

✗

LOST IN TRANSLATION

by John M. Floyd

At eight a.m. Sheriff Lucy Valentine and her crimefighting mother Fran climbed out of Lucy's cruiser and approached the front entrance of the local middle school. Fran took a deep breath and looked around. "Memory lane," she said. "It feels good."

Lucy snorted. "For you, maybe. You were a teacher here—I was a student."

"You were a troublemaker," Fran reminded her. "Remember the time you hit Mr. Pearson with an eraser in the auditorium, during his speech?"

"I didn't hit nobody with a eraser."

"I didn't hit *any*body with an eraser," Fran corrected.

"Well, that makes two of us." The sheriff stopped just inside the front doors and checked her notepad. "Let's see…I was told to go to the principal's office."

"Some things never change," Fran said dryly.

The two of them found the principal—Ms. Logan—waiting at her desk. After greeting Fran and thanking Lucy for coming, Logan said, "I'll get right to the point, Sheriff: I received an anonymous call at my home this morning informing me that some new computer equipment was stolen from our school last night."

"And how did this caller know about it?" Lucy asked, easing into one of the two visitors' chairs.

"She saw a man in a janitor's uniform sneaking it out the door."

"Uniform?"

"Gray coveralls, actually, with the school emblem."

Fran frowned, thinking. "How many janitors are here after hours?"

"Three." The principal spread three personnel sheets out on the desktop, complete with head shots. "Alex Martinez, Jerry Smith, and Lawrence Robertson."

Both Fran and the sheriff leaned forward to study the photos. Martinez had long black hair, a thick mustache, a round face, and an oversized nose; Smith had pale skin, a scar on his cheek, and sandy hair; Robertson, an African American, had a shaved head and a square chin. In appearance, the three men couldn't have been more different.

"And this nameless informant saw only one person?" Lucy asked.

"That's right. She said she looked out her window around midnight and saw a janitor carry three stacked boxes of laptop computers out the south door of the school."

"How'd she know they were laptops?"

"Said she could see the pictures on the boxes."

"If she saw this from a window," Lucy said, settling back into her chair, "maybe we could locate and question her."

"Doubtful." Principal Logan steepled her fingers under her chin as if praying. "There are two apartment buildings across the street from that entrance, Sheriff Valentine. That's a lot of windows."

"How about her phone number? You don't have caller ID?"

"Not on my landline, at home."

Lucy stayed quiet a moment, then asked the big question. "You think she was telling the truth?"

"Well, she said she saw three boxes, and we've verified that three laptops are missing. They'd only just been delivered, and never even taken out of their boxes."

"Anything else? Did the caller identify which janitor it was?"

"In a way. After she told me what she'd seen, I heard—in the background—another lady's voice asking her that very question: 'Who was it?' The first woman answered, 'It was *him*. I recognized his car.'"

Lucy sat up a little straighter, eyes narrowed. "His car?"

"Those were her exact words. 'I recognized his car.' Then she hung up."

"What does that tell you?"

"More than you might think." Principal Logan pointed to the three folders. "You see, only one of these three janitors—Alex Martinez—has a car. A bright yellow Toyota, maybe thirty years old. Pretty unique." A pause. "One of the others—Smith—drives an old pickup truck, not a car, and the third—Larry Robertson—always walks the half mile to work and back, from Oak Street."

Sheriff Valentine spread her hands. "So Martinez is the thief?"

The principal sighed. "It's not that simple. My assistant's husband works at a body shop downtown, and knows Alex. He'd told her that Alex Martinez brought his yellow Toyota in with hail damage three days ago. She phoned her husband first thing this morning, when I asked her to, to confirm that. The car's still there." She shrugged. "Which leaves us with nothing."

"Well," Lucy said, "I can get phone records. That would tell us what number called yours this morning, and if we then get a home address from that and find and question the caller, we could—hopefully—get the name of who she saw, or thought she saw. But if she'd wanted to reveal the name, why didn't she just give it to you on the phone? And obtaining those records can take time. The stolen goods will almost certainly be resold by then, and—"

"I don't think you'll have to do that," Fran said.

The others turned to look at her. "Excuse me?" the principal said.

Fran, who was squinting in a way that her daughter knew well, replied, "I think I know who stole your computers, Ms. Logan."

"But—how?"

"Have you ever heard anybody tell someone something, and the person hearing it gets an entirely different meaning from what was intended?"

"Of course. Sometimes that's the plot basis for TV sitcoms."

"Well, I think that's what happened here," Fran said. "I think your informant told the truth, and I'm sure you told us what you heard."

"But…?"

"I don't think what you heard was what she actually said. I mean, she couldn't have recognized 'his car,' right? Apparently none of them *had* a car, that night."

The principal did a palms-up. "So, if that's true—who *was* the thief?"

"Think about it," Fran said. "I believe what the caller really said was: 'I recognized his *scar*.'"

The room went quiet. Ms. Logan's eyes widened.

"Jerry Smith," Logan said.

Fran nodded. "The only one of the three who has a scar. On his face and in plain view."

Lucy was staring as well, but recovered quickly. She fished her cell phone from her pocket, punched a number, and—after reading aloud the address information from the personnel sheet—directed her deputy to pick up Mr. Smith in connection with a burglary at the middle school. When she disconnected, she took a long breath, looked at her mother, and smiled. "Well done, my dear Watson."

"Elementary," Fran said.

After standing and exchanging thanks all around, and as Fran and Lucy were turning to leave, Principal Logan said, "Sheriff Valentine?"

Lucy paused, waiting.

"I must tell you," Logan said, "you've turned out much better than I ever thought, back when you were a student here."

"Thanks," Lucy said. "I guess."

"You guess?"

"I'm trying to figure out if that was a compliment."

The principal grinned. "Me too."

When Fran and Lucy were outside and on the way to their car, Fran stopped in her tracks. Lucy turned to look at her. "What's the matter?"

"I just remembered," Fran said. "That day you threw the eraser in assembly? It wasn't Mr. Pearson you hit. It was another teacher."

"Who?"

"Ms. Logan."

Lucy was silent a moment, then nodded. "I think you're right." Deep in thought, she continued walking toward the patrol car.

Fran couldn't help smiling as she followed.

"So much for Memory Lane," she said.

"DIAMONDS"

by Kelli A. Wilkins

Vinnie heard the barking as soon as he stepped out of the car. He unlocked the back door to the blue house and strolled into the kitchen, ignoring the eager-looking beagle he was supposed to feed.

He wandered through the small Cape-Cod style home, surveyed the furnishings, and shrugged. Middle class. Ordinary. Sometimes he got lucky, sometimes not. Either way, he had a pretty decent racket going. According to the stat sheet his cousin Louie had given him, Maggie Collins would be out of town until Tuesday.

As a part-time worker for his cousin's pet-sitting service, he was able to case houses, pick up whatever spare cash might be lying around, find jewelry to pawn, and even watch cable TV.

The pet-sitting assignments kept him busy in several counties, and he made sure never to hit more than one house per town. Usually he lifted small objects that no one would miss right away. Some people owned so much crap that they never noticed when things went missing.

Last month, he had found an antique silver tea set buried under some junk in the corner of a client's basement. He'd pawned it for $300. That made a nice bonus for feeding Fido and Fluffy.

He hooked his thumbs into the belt loops of his jeans and sauntered down the narrow hallway. The beagle raced past him and started scratching at a closed door. The hound looked up at him and let out a short bark.

"Shut up, mutt!" he snapped. The dog was probably hungry, but it would have to wait until he was good and ready to feed it. He had more important things to tend to first. As soon as he had cased the house, he'd grab something to eat from the fridge and watch a few movies.

He paused in the hallway and read the inscription on a gold-framed plaque hanging on the wall. 'Margaret Collins: Herpetologist of the Year.'

He frowned. He'd heard that word before, on a game show or something, but he couldn't remember what it meant. It wasn't anything important, because she obviously wasn't rich. His cousin had told him that this Collins woman was a teacher at the local college.

The beagle barked again. "Come on, dog. Let's get you fed so you'll shut up already."

Vinnie tugged on the beagle's collar and dragged it into the blue and white kitchen. He opened a can of dog food and slapped it down in a metal dish just as the phone rang. The answering machine recorded the message as he rummaged around in the refrigerator. Didn't this woman have any beer?

"Hi Maggie. This is Joe. I know you're not home, but I wanted to let you know that I'll stop over on Wednesday to pick up those diamonds. Call me when you get in."

A tingle ran down his spine. "Diamonds?" He grinned as he straightened up and closed the refrigerator. And just when he'd written this house off…

He hurried down the hallway and tried to open one of the closed doors. It was locked. He let out a little laugh. Indoor locks, why did people even bother? Vinnie DeCarlo was a burglary professional with over fifteen years of experience. There wasn't a locked door that he couldn't get behind.

He liked to think that even though every house posed some kind of challenge to him, he'd find a way to win and get what he deserved. After nearly getting caught a few times, he had thought about going straight, but that required too much work. A legit job wouldn't pay as good as this sweet deal did. This was easy and quick. Besides, he always got a thrill out of rummaging through other people's lives. He never knew what sort of interesting things he'd find.

Within seconds, he had picked the cheap lock and stepped inside the bedroom. He heard a plaintive whine and cast a glance behind him. The beagle had abandoned its dinner and stood in the hallway with its head cocked to one side, watching him.

"Some guard dog you are. Go lay down," he snapped.

He turned back and surveyed the room. Margaret Collins's bedroom was ordinary, except for the large walk-in closet that took up a corner of the room. Vinnie opened the wooden jewelry box perched on the dresser and rooted through it.

What kind of diamonds did she have? A pair of earrings? A bracelet? An engagement ring? His mind raced with the possibilities of what he could buy with the loot. A down payment on a decent car…a 60-inch television…

As soon as he stashed the jewels, he'd come back and make it look like someone had broken in and trashed the place. Everyone knew that most break-ins happened when people were away on vacation or business. He'd call the cops and pretend to be concerned. The simple story would sell. He'd explain that he came over to feed the dog, saw what had happened, and phoned it in.

A loud yap interrupted his thoughts. The beagle stood just outside the bedroom door, barking. He scowled. Maybe that annoying dog would have an "accident" while the house was being robbed. "Get lost!" He slammed the bedroom door in the dog's face.

Vinnie rifled through the dresser drawers and the nightstand. Nothing. He sighed and looked around the room. The diamonds had to be somewhere. His gaze fell on the partially open closet door. Of course! People always hid things in the closet.

He stepped into the huge walk-in and furrowed his brows. What the hell? This was strange. The walls were lined with large glass tanks supported on wooden shelves. He ignored the still-barking dog and inched closer. The tanks looked like they were filled with rocks and sand. What was this Collins broad doing with these?

Vinnie leaned over and tapped the grated metal cover on the nearest tank. A tan pile of "rocks" snapped up its triangular-shaped head and flicked a dark, forked tongue at him. He yelped and jumped back.

Now he remembered! Herpetologists studied snakes! He hated snakes. They were nasty, slimy creatures. Maggie Collins must be keeping these hideous things in here while she was away for the long weekend.

His arms broke out in goosebumps as he gazed at the tanks filled with serpents. In the dim light, he saw several pale round things half-buried beneath the sand. Were they eggs? He knew from watching those boring documentaries on television that animals got pissed off if they thought someone was trying to steal their eggs.

"Just stay cool. Don't panic," he whispered. He took a deep breath and held it in for a second. His heart hammered out of control, and he licked a droplet of sweat off his upper lip. All he had to do was act calm and get the hell out of here before those things got any more riled up. If the diamonds were hidden in these tanks, they could stay right where they were.

He jumped as the beagle howled outside the bedroom door. How the frig was he supposed to stay calm when that damn dog was raising hell?

Vinnie kept his gaze riveted on the tanks. His eyes had adjusted to the dim light, and now he could see the creatures clearly. They slithered through the sand with their heads raised and their tongues flicking the air in front of them.

His knees wobbled as he backed toward the closet door. He kicked something metal and sent it clattering across the wood floor. His entire body broke out in a cold sweat as he realized what the object was. "Don't even tell me that was one of the—"

He froze as he heard a chilling rattle from the shelf just above his head. He glanced up and swallowed hard. Tiny, coal-black eyes were fixed on him in a deadly stare. Before he could make a sound, the tan and black serpent reared back and struck hard.

He felt a quick sting as the fangs punctured his neck. He crumpled forward against the other tanks and finally understood. He had found the diamonds he came looking for—Diamondback Rattlers!

✗

IN MEMORIAM: A VIGNETTE

by Stan Trybulski

He was up before the early summer sun peeped over the mountains. He was ready to work and after scrounging through his desk he found a pencil with a worn nub still good enough to write with. He sat at his desk and tried but it was no use. He knew the story would have been a good story, but he couldn't write it because even though he had once worked it all out in his head, he couldn't quite remember what it was about and how it would end. They had stolen it from him, the doctors with their electricity and the FBI with their microphones and cameras; the lousy bastards had stolen all of it, scooping it out of the coils of his mind like robbers grabbing money from a bank till.

In a fit of anger, he threw the pencil across the room and, still in his bare feet, padded downstairs to the kitchen in search of a drink, only to find himself taking a ring of keys on the windowsill and going on down to the cellar. He went to the storeroom and unlocked it and took out two twelve-gauge shells and his favorite Boss shotgun. It was then that he remembered what the story was about and that, like all the others, it was about him. They had not stolen it from him after all, he swore. They would be back to try again, but he would never let them get it.

He loaded the Boss and took it back upstairs. Setting the gunstock on the floor, he placed the mouths of the barrels under his chin. He wriggled his big toe through the trigger housing, suddenly laughing, because now he also remembered how the story was supposed to end. His big toe found the two little pieces of curled steel and as he pushed down, he laughed again, knowing that he no longer needed the pencil with its worn nub. This was the one thing he couldn't get rid of on paper.

✗

Stan Trybulski is the author of the popular Doherty series and was a felony trial prosecutor for the district attorney's office in Brooklyn and later a civil trial attorney for the New York City Department of Education. Prior to becoming an attorney, Trybulski was a newspaper reporter, college administrator, bartender, and a long-time frequenter of McSorley's Old Ale House in New York City. During his legal career, he made McSorley's his office away from the office, and has continued that tradition through his writing career, using the front table as his desk, its cats as his editorial assistants, and the tavern as a locale in his novels and short stories.

THE MYSTERY OF THE MISSING MONEY

by Mary Laufer

An elderly woman opened the front door and beckoned two visitors to come in. Detective Jennifer Hamilton slipped off her shoes, but her partner, Detective Chad Morris, strutted in behind her without removing his muddy oxfords. Hamilton scowled and elbowed him in the ribs. After all, Clara Firestine was a victim of a crime, and they shouldn't add to her problems by staining her nice carpet. According to the report, someone had stolen $5,000 from the woman.

"I'm so glad you're here," Mrs. Firestine said in a creaky voice. "I've been shaking like a leaf ever since I realized my money was gone."

The detectives followed her into the living room. The frail woman leaned on a cane and walked slightly bent over, her gray head bobbing with every step. She stopped in front of a wooden rocker and with the help of the cane slowly lowered herself to a sitting position.

"Please have a seat," she said, pointing toward the couch. "Would you like a cup of tea? How about a chocolate chip cookie?"

Hamilton detected the pleasant aroma of freshly baked cookies. "No, thank you," she said as she sat down. She glanced at Morris with a suppressed smile. "Would you like something, Chad?"

"No, thanks," Morris said, taking a pen and a pad of paper out of his leather briefcase. "If you don't mind, ma'am, we'd like to get started with our investigation."

"Oh, that's right," Mrs. Firestine said. "For a minute, I forgot why you were here!"

Morris cleared his throat. "Why don't you show us where the money was taken from."

Mrs. Firestine struggled to stand up. She led the detectives to the hall closet and pushed aside the long coats with her cane, revealing a small black safe. "It was closed and locked the day I discovered my money gone," she said. "I still can't understand how the thief figured out the combination."

Morris knelt on one knee and examined the safe. "It doesn't appear to have been tampered with," he said. He went to his briefcase and pulled out a fingerprint kit.

As Morris tried to lift prints, Hamilton turned to Mrs. Firestine and asked, "Does anyone besides you know the combination to the safe?"

"My husband Elmer did, but he died last year," Mrs. Firestine said sadly. "He knew how forgetful I was, so he wrote the combination on the back of our wedding picture."

She picked up a silver-framed photograph from the mantel, turned it over, and brought it near her face. "Good thing I can still see things close to my nose," she laughed.

"May I?' Hamilton asked. Mrs. Firestine handed her the picture, and she inspected the back of the frame. Written in one corner was a string of five numbers. "Has anyone new been in your home recently?" Hamilton asked. "Someone who may have been left alone in your living room with this photograph for a little while? A repairman maybe? Or a salesman?"

"I don't get many visitors," the woman explained. "Only my children and grandchildren. They wouldn't have taken the money. I'm sure of that. And then there's Rosemary. She comes to clean for a couple hours every Friday morning. But she's an honest girl."

Morris raised his eyebrows. "Does Rosemary dust your photographs?" he asked.

"Why, yes. She dusts the whole house." A moment of silence passed, and then the detective's accusation registered. Mrs. Firestine's eyes widened. "Rosemary didn't steal the money!" she cried. "That sweet girl has been working for me for five years." She looked away. "Or has it been ten?"

"It's okay, Clara. We believe you," Hamilton said, patting the woman's arm. "Just one more question. How did you come to have so much cash in your house? Why wasn't it in a bank?"

Mrs. Firestine sighed. "I've never trusted banks. Each month when I cashed my social security check, I saved some of the money out and tucked it away in the safe. I planned to buy new carpet. My grandchildren have run this old carpet ragged."

Hamilton gazed down at the floor and frowned. The only signs of traffic in the plush burgundy carpet were impressions of their feet and round marks from the woman's cane.

Just then, a shrill whistle came from the kitchen. "Oh, that's my tea kettle!" Mrs. Firestine exclaimed. "I forgot I put it on the stove right before you came. Would either of you like a cup of tea? How about a chocolate chip cookie?"

"No, thank you," the detectives said at the same time.

Mrs. Firestine shuffled off as fast as she could to the other room. When she was out of hearing range, Morris whispered to Hamilton, "My bet is on the cleaning woman. She could be preying on the elderly. Let's check her out and see if she has other clients who are missing valuables."

Deep in thought, Hamilton stared at the flawless carpet. Suddenly she broke out in a grin, as if the answer had occurred to her. "That won't be necessary. Neither will the fingerprints. I think I know who took the money."

Morris shrugged. "Who?"

"Clara Firestine," Hamilton whispered.

"Huh?"

"Look at the carpet. Does it appear ragged to you?"

Morris scanned the floor and shook his head. "It's brand new." His eyes lit up. "You think she just forgot?"

"Shhh!" Hamilton said.

Mrs. Firestine hobbled around the corner, a plate of cookies in her hand. "Would either of you be interested in a chocolate chip cookie?" she asked. "How about a cup of tea?"

"I'd love a homemade cookie," Hamilton said, reaching out and taking one from the plate. "But we'd better be careful not to get crumbs on your nice carpet. Is it new?"

"Oh, yes," Mrs. Firestine said. "I just had it put in two weeks ago. Beautiful, isn't it? I got it on sale. What a steal! You'd never guess how much it cost."

✗

PEA SOUP

by Gerald Elias

"Sure! On a day like this it's easy to feel like a million bucks. Look at that! The bluest sky on God's earth! And look at them trees! There's nothing like sugar maples, with their yellows and their oranges. And look! Look up there! See those reds on top? And that air! Go ahead. Breathe it in real good. Trample on those leaves—yeah, crunch 'em—and you'll smell it coming right out of the earth. And that sun! You've got your chill in the air but that sun, it warms you up. Apple-pickin' weather. Makes you feel alive. What can be better, right? Right? Well sure, the days're fine, but it's when the sun goes down, that's when I get the jitters. When that chill creeps in and all the color becomes shades of gray and then the gray disappears and there's only black and then you can't even see the blackness. It sneaks in quiet. There was this dandy that lived down the road for a while—from Europe, I think—who wrote fancy poetry. I don't know what happened to him—maybe he finally had to get a job—but I remember him reciting one of his poems, you know, in that dandified tone poets like to talk in—about New England fog that gave me the heebie-jeebies. I've never forgotten it: 'The unsettling assassin who settles in like damp death.' Don't get me wrong. I'm no poet—do I look like a poet?—and New England weather, it never bothered me none nevermind—not the blizzards, not the green-sky thunderstorms, not even the below-zero winters that go on and on and end up with two months of 'mud season' before things finally turn green. But that damned fog. You can't shovel it. You can't pump it out. You can't even touch it. It just wraps itself around you. Around everything. Just about strangles you. The fog makes my skin crawl. I'm not the only one in my extended family so afflicted; it's almost as much a family tradition as our Thanksgiving pea soup. You'd think a family that's been in Massachusetts since a hundred fifty years before the Revolution would've gotten used to the fog by now. The fog, that's one of the two traits that've plagued our family. The other, the mental illness, isn't so curious or harmless, if you will—you see more and more of it these days—though we've pretended it's not there and act like everything is just hunky-dory—'communal denial' is what a psychiatrist once told me it was called. Thank the Lord I've been spared. If you did one of those genealogies like my cousin Rachel did, going back to when our progenitors first set their roots here in Cromwell in 1624, you'd see that the family tree that grew out of it looks more like the back roads of the Berkshires—you think you're going off in one direction but then you get twisted around in the woods for a while and you find that you've just crisscrossed the same road you started out on. That the Buttmans and the Caines and the Oglebees likely exchanged their nocturnal whatevers up there on Taylor Hill Road and other hidden lanes makes the metaphor more than a passing one. They say one of these days they're going to pave Taylor Hill Road."

"Metaphor?" asked Fisk, jotting down the word.

"Well, you know what I mean. With that level of family togetherness it's a wonder there haven't been even more clan fruitcakes roaming the woods. This intermarriage thing—well, it's no big surprise for a small town; probably no different in Africa or Mongolia—but here in the Four Towns area which has been rural since we gave the Indians the old heave-ho, I wouldn't be surprised if somehow just about everyone is related to each other in some fashion. Uncle Abel, who kind of pooh-poohed Rachel, once handed her the Four Towns phone book and said, 'Honey, that's all the genealogy you'll ever need.' Rachel didn't think the joke was too funny but then again she never did have much of a sense of humor. Among the kinfolk the most prevalent mental illness—other than fear of fog—has been the seizures. They started to show as early as the beginning of the eighteen-hundreds—probably even sooner—and hopped around to various branches of the family. I know about this because Rachel dredged up a document from 1819 about a certain gentleman relation named Erasmus Sharp, or Sharpp—spelling was not very consistent in those days—while doing one of her fancy-ass Internet searches. I've never had a computer myself, but here it is—she made a copy of the original for me, and put in the corrections. Here, take a look. Kind of hard to read, being hand-scrawled."

Fisk read it aloud.

"'[Erasmus] did Tremble and Shake in so violent a manner that we were compelled [*sic*] to pacify him with stout chord and strength of arm to prevent him from doing harm unto himself and unto others thereby. We were sorely troubled by his choleric Humor, but neither balm nor bleeding brought the sought [for] relief. Only time, fatigue, and Faith in the Almighty restored our brother to his senses. We pray that his Affliction will not return so soon.'"

"Hey, give me that!"

Fisk handed it back.

"Then there were my three-hundred-fifty-pound second cousins, about eighteen times removed, Ezekiel and Zachariah, aka Zeke and Zack, who were in the habit of promenading naked down Main Street in East Sagcutt. No polite urging dissuaded them from their proclivity, so finally they were hauled off to a work farm. Having to sweat twelve hours a day in a field quickly reformed their ways."

Fisk wrote down 'dissuaded.' And 'proclivity.'

"I only mention all this because of what happened to Uncle Abel. I had just finished packing my bags when the call from Cousin Rachel came. I was getting ready to move because, to tell you the truth, I'd been worn down by New England. Tired of dampness, tired of darkness, and yes, the aforementioned fog. I'm heading to Arizona where the sun doth shine and where I won't have to wait until Memorial Day to plant my tomatoes just to see them rot on the vine from frost two months later. I won't have to split firewood just to wait a year 'til it's seasoned enough to burn without sparking a creosote fire in my chimney. I won't have to break my back shoveling snow so's to get out of the driveway so's to buy a space heater so's to keep the pipes in my cellar from freezing! A long overdue new start, wouldn't you say? So when a school in Phoenix accepted me into their master's program it was an omen sent from heaven. But when Rachel told me Uncle Abel died I had no choice except to put a hold on the plans. Even in a family that populates most of several small towns—a 'simple' majority, you might say—a death amongst us is no laughing matter. It wouldn't look good if I just headed out of Dodge and to tell you the truth there was something special about Uncle Abel. Uncle Abel, sadly, had been one of the afflicted, and not just the seizures. Uncle Abel had been incarcerated for crimes of violence. None of his offenses resulted in anyone being killed, mind you, but over time they'd gotten more aggravated, a cause of some concern to the family. It started with farm animals a long time ago, then turned to humans. He beat someone pretty badly with a hoe for no apparent reason. The prosecutor said it was a shovel, but it really was only a hoe. After doing time, they sent Uncle Abel to a mental health facility, then a halfway house, and finally, after copious rehabilitation, he was—according to his parole board, anyway—deemed fit to be released back into society. Since then, and we're talking years now, he lived in tranquility in Cromwell, content to be left alone in the house where he'd growed up. Great-great-grandfather Josiah Buttman built that house in 1849 upon the occasion of his marriage to his teenage bride, Mehitabel. Or so Rachel tells me. You couldn't build a house like that now, there not being a right angle in the place and nothing would be up to code. You just have to take a look at—"

"Could you stick to the subject, please?" asked Fisk.

"I just was trying to make the point that—and I'm not denying he had his foibles—I always felt Uncle Abel was a good man. I should mention that Cromwell—it's officially a town but it doesn't have a town center or village green to speak of, and there's no commerce except for a cousin who's an auto mechanic on Lane Road. Cromwell's basically just a big chunk of land dotted here and there with houses. Used to be almost all farms, but the past fifty years or so the forests have snuck back in; they've swallowed up the cornfields and the pasture, making things even more isolated. Claustrophobic, you could say. Folks pretty much keep to themselves and Uncle Abel's place was about as far off the beaten track as you could get. His property and the state forest was butted up together like Siamese twins. The one thing Uncle Abel took pride in was the pond right next to his house. When he was a young man, so he liked to tell, the pond was just a slimy depression in the ground and water seeped up from underneath every spring and then dried out by the end of the summer. On a whim, Uncle Abel decided why not dig it out a bit to see what'd happen. Turned out the water table was yea high in that one spot—which was odd because some of his nearest neighbors had to dig down three-, four-hundred foot to sink a well—and Uncle Able's hole filled with water pretty darn quick. And the more he dug the faster the hole filled, getting deeper and darker, deeper and darker. You can see for yourself how big the pond is now—bigger than the house even—and it's a good eight feet deep in its center. How Uncle Abel managed to shovel that out without drowning will take someone smarter than me to figure out. He surrounded the pond with some big rocks to make it look natural. Little by little ferns and other plants grew, then the worms—there was tons of worms—and frogs came, and the birds came, and the deer came, and even a bobcat or two. He caught a few fish in a nearby creek and released them into the pond, and they must've been pretty happy fellas and gals because they bred faster than the Buttmans and the Caines. The bank of the pond migrated so far, Uncle Abel could fish right from his own porch. Unfortunately, as you know, that's where they also found Uncle Abel. Floating in his pond with his fish. He had one of his intermittent seizures, fell over the porch railing, hit his head on a rock and drowned. At least that's what the preliminary police report said."

Fisk looked up from his notes.

"Anyway, they buried Uncle Abel in the Cromwell graveyard alongside the rest of our illustrious ancestors and the family pow-wowed at the Grange Hall in East Sagcutt to decide what to do with his house and possessions. I should mention that, Uncle Abel having been such a hermit and never having married or having off-spring—that we know of—his house became something of a shack and his possessions were more in the nature of—to be perfectly honest—junk. Except for one thing that I'll mention in a moment. We came to a pretty easy decision to sell the property. No doubt the house'll be torn down, but the land is valuable—it's good land—especially being adjacent to the state forest. Some nice upwardly mobile couple will build a big modern house on the land and raise a bunch of snotty, pampered kids. Who knows, they might even turn out to be some of our relatives. Of Uncle Abel's belongings, after family members chose something to remember him by, we'd donate what was usable to the Goodwill; the rest we'd throw out. Over the years there'd been a rumor that Uncle Abel had in his possession a box of family letters and documents dating from co-lonial times, the contents of which would be interesting history especially for Rachel, but I was told that the stamps on the letters would fetch a pretty penny particularly since they were suppos-edly still on the original envelopes. Plus, it was rumored, there was a certificate signed by George Washington discharging one of our distinguished great-great-greats from the Continental army and deeding him a land grant upon the termination of the Revolution. When I arrived at the Buttman homestead in the afternoon it was one of them perfect late fall New England days and there was relations like a bunch of ants scouring the place to the bone. It didn't seem totally right to me. Cousin Rachel had an old carton of empty Moxie bottles squeezed to her chest and was trying to snake by me. 'Are you sure it's okay doing this?' I asked. 'Doing what?' she asked me. 'This is what we all decided.' I said 'I don't know. It feels kind of weird. Some of this might be evidence.' 'Evidence of what?' she asked me. I said 'Well, you know, the way Uncle Abel died.' Rachel said 'Spencer, it was an accident.' I said 'Well, it *looked* like an accident. I'll grant you that. But who knows what *really* happened? It was pea soup fog the night he died. Maybe it wasn't a seizure. Maybe someone walked in unseen and hit Uncle Abel in the head, and threw him into the pond to look like an accident.' 'Why would anyone have done that?' Rachel said. 'He'd kept to himself for years and no one ever bothered him. He'd paid his dues.' I asked her 'What about the stamps?' Do you know what old stamps are worth?"

Fisk looked up to see that the question was directed at him. He shook his head.

"No, I don't."

"I've been told they're not hard to sell, though why people will pay a lot of money for little pieces of old paper and dried glue is beyond me. I guess that's human nature. Rachel asked me back 'What stamps, Spencer? We've torn the place apart looking for "the treasure" and the most valuable thing we've found is a box of Harry Truman campaign buttons.' I said 'Well, maybe they took the stamps.' 'So it's *they* now?' Rachel said. She was starting to sound pedantic to me. I said 'You know what I mean.' Rachel said 'Spencer, I love you dearly, but you're sounding like a crazy conspiracy theorist. The police were here. They investigated. They said as far as they could tell nothing had been disturbed.' '*As far as they could tell!*' I said. That did it. Rachel said 'Oh, Spencer! Go make yourself useful. Grab a keepsake. We have to empty the place by the end of the day.' And then she walked away from me, ignoring that I was still pretty shaken up. I wandered around the house, touching the stone fireplace that always had a backdraft no matter what; the oak rocking chair with arms that'd turned black with wear; the painting on the wall of someone whose name I never knew. This would be the last time I'd be here; 'here' being not just Uncle Abel's place but New England. The sun was already starting to set—the days get so damn short this time of year you wonder if they were really there—and I could feel that fog already getting under my skin even before I could see it. On my way out I noticed the paperweight on the kitchen counter. I was a little taken aback to see it still sitting right there, but relieved no kin had yet claimed it for a souvenir. It was on the Four Towns phone book next to the stockpot of pea soup that Rachel had cooked to keep the troops happy as they cleaned out the house. Family secret for generations, that pea soup recipe; ham hock, potato, onion, bay leaves, salt, pepper. Just a smidge was left thickening in the pot. I poked my finger through the scum that was getting crusty on top and licked it off. It's a nice old paperweight, a real collector's item, not one of those cheap plastic jobs with fake snow and a tacky winter scene of a tree and a snowman. You know Norman Rockwell? You know his famous painting of Main Street in Stockbridge? This one's a 3D replica and very nicely done. Instead of snow when you shake it, red and yellow and orange leaves flutter around and then settle on the ground. On the outside of it, which is heavy-duty glass of a kind they don't make anymore, with a solid maple base, it reads 'Welcome to the Berkshires, 1949.' A little world of its own inside that glass. A perfect autumn day from a perfect era and all you have to do is shake it. I looked around and picked up the paperweight and slid it into my pocket and left the house and smiled and waved and promised everyone I'd stay in touch. By the time I got to the car, the sun was already low, below the trees. It made my shadow look like some creepy monster. I started my car—they waved 'Good-bye, Spencer'—but I didn't look back. I sped off before the fog could catch up to me."

"Abel," said Detective Fisk.

"Huh?"

"What's your name? Tell me your name."

"Spencer? Isn't it?"

"No, it's not. It's Abel. Abel Buttman."

"Abel?"

"That's right. You are Abel Buttman. Abel, do you know what words like 'proclivity' and 'metaphor' and 'dissuaded' mean?"

"Not really. No. Well, sort of. I've heard them bandied about now and then. Why?"

"Because you just used those big words in your statement."

"I did? Huh!"

"Yes, you did. Those are the kind of words a college graduate would use, aren't they? As far as we know, Abel, you never graduated junior high."

"Nah. Who has time for that rubbish?"

"But they might be the kind of words your great-nephew Spencer might have used with you. Might they not?"

"I'm not Spencer?"

"No, Abel," said Detective Fisk. "You're not Spencer. Abel, I'm now going to walk you through what *actually* happened.

"You, Abel Buttman, murdered your great-nephew Spencer Caine, by bludgeoning him with the paperweight—"

"That's a real collector's item."

"Yes it is, Abel. Particularly for us, because we found ample traces of Spencer's blood, scalp, and skull fragments on the paperweight and in your jacket pocket in which it was found. Since you were alone in your house it's hard to imagine that someone else put it there. Is it not true, Abel Buttman, that after Spencer was dead—after you, Abel Buttman, killed him—you dragged him across your porch, as the scuff marks on the deck boards that match Spencer's shoes would indicate, and lowered him into your pond, hoping his body would go undiscovered?"

"He was going to steal my stamps. They're worth a lot of money. A *helluva* lot of money."

"Abel, Spencer came to your house with Rachel," said Detective Fisk. "Spencer wanted to say good-bye because he was moving to Phoenix to go back to college. There are no stamps, Abel. There never were any stamps."

"No? No stamps? Well, everything gets kinda foggy. It was a foggy night. Pea soup! Are you sure there weren't any stamps?"

"No, Abel. No stamps. Let's start over, shall we?"

"All over?"

"Yes. All over. You were telling me about apple-picking season in New England. Tell me again about apple-picking season, Abel, and this time around maybe you'll also be kind enough to tell me what you've done with Rachel."

"Sure! On a day like this it's easy to feel like a million bucks…"

PLAYING FOR KEEPS

by Meg Opperman

Dar es Salaam, Tanzania

The gentle breeze blowing in from the ocean gave Lucky Kajage much needed relief from Dar's scorching heat. He paused in his work at the Daladala[1] Bar to swipe his pale yellow dreadlocks away from his damp face and neck, tying them up with one of his braids. January in Dar es Salaam was a killer, but at least he'd make rent this month. He returned to shoveling the empty plates and beer bottles onto a small tray, then ran a damp cloth over the tabletop's sticky surface. As he wiped, he hunkered beneath the table's thatched umbrella. Albinos in Tanzania typically didn't survive long under the sun's cancerous rays. He planned to be an exception.

A shadow fell across the table.

Lucky squinted, trying to identify the silhouette.

"Hey, hey, wazzup, Lucky? How's everyone's favorite *mzungu[2]?*" said a rapid-fire voice.

Lucky knew the meter—urban youth—but couldn't place the pitch. He blinked to clear the sunspots from his vision.

The figure yanked out a chair and dropped into it.

Rostam Zambi. Lucky grimaced.

"Original, *broo[3]*. Hadn't heard that one before." *Mzungu*—a white person? He'd only gotten that joke about a thousand times. Nothing like being a walking punchline.

"Just jokin' you, *braza[4]*," Rostam said, clasping Lucky in a three-move handshake.

"No worries. Worse things to be called than a white person. Second-rate hack, for example." Lucky smiled, his other hand

---

1   Locally owned buses.

2   White person, someone of European origin. In the story's context, used derogatorily to refer to Lucky's albinism.

3   Bro, brother (slang).

4   Brother (slang).

squeezing the cleaning rag so hard that water trickled down his wrist.

"Funny, Lucky. Good one." Settling back, Rostam pulled a small, ebony box with a tiny keyhole on the side from his shirt pocket and set it on the table, then reached back in his pocket and drew out a half-smoked cigarette and matches. He lit up and puffed energetically. "Didn't 'spect to see you servin' beer and shit. Times is tough for you guys, no?"

"You ordering something?" Lucky didn't meet Rostam's gaze. Local musicians and their hangers-on gathered at the Daladala Bar, so he'd had lots of regulars say the same thing. He still hadn't come up with a clever reply. "The calamari's good today. Fresh caught, and Mama Kimari herself is working the grill."

"Take a break. I'll buy a round." Rostam's fingers tapped a beat on the box, all nervous energy.

"I'm working for a couple of hours yet. I'll bring you a beer, though."

Rostam's fingers stilled. "Kilimanjaro, then. Warm. And I'll take some of that calamari. Extra lime and hot pepper."

Lucky shouldered his tray and retreated to the old, gutted bus that gave the Daladala Bar its name. It housed a large grill and numerous crates of beer. He slipped in between a couple of shapely waitresses, their movements slow and easy as they hoisted heavy trays. After dumping the empty dishes and bottles, he called in Rostam's order. Mama Kimari plated another bunch of calamari and slid them onto the ledge of the bus.

She glanced at Lucky, ran her arm over her dripping forehead. "When's Kim coming? Maybe he'd be willing to help out."

Her comment made Lucky snort. Then both of them broke into a fit of laughter. Mama Kimari's little brother—and the lead singer in Lucky's band—would never stoop to waiting tables. Not good for his image. Simon "Kim" Kimari didn't even like Lucky doing it, but a man had to pay his bills. And playing guitar just didn't cut it these days.

"I needed that, thanks," Lucky said.

Mama Kimari gave him a kind smile, her unusual blue eyes the twins of Kim's own. "Know this is hard on you, Lucky. And," she pointed with her chin to Rostam, "these kids only make it worse."

Lucky shrugged and glanced at Rostam out of the corner of his eye. Just another bongoland[5] kid sporting low-slung jeans, a sideways-facing cap, and calling himself a guitarist. Hooligan chic. The untidy style had infected much of Dar's youth, although Lucky couldn't imagine why. Wasn't it uncomfortable having trousers practically wrapped around one's ankles? His finger traced the crease painstakingly ironed into his own denim, so sharp it could almost draw blood.

A waitress jostled him reaching for her food, and he sprang back into action. He scooped a plate of calamari and a beer onto his tray. Remembering the extra lime and hot peppers, he ferried the order back to Rostam and carefully set everything down. He stood, waiting for payment.

Rostam stubbed out his cigarette on the sole of his newly minted Nike-knockoffs, his other hand spinning the small box like a top. "You interested in playin' on another CD? Good money in it." Rostam pointed to a chair across from him.

Lucky didn't know what to make of that. Before he could sit, a regular at another table whistled and held up his empty bottle. "Give me a minute," Lucky said.

✗　✗　✗　✗

For the next hour, Lucky hustled from table to table. As the afternoon wore on, more customers filed in. He must have hauled ten crates worth of beer to various tables.

At the first lull, he circled back to Rostam and eased into a seat. He noticed a soggy pile of shillings held down by an empty beer bottle. Wincing, he gathered the bills, and made change. Then tugging a bandana out of his pocket, he wiped his face. "What's this about a CD, *broo*?" Did he sound too desperate?

"First, *hongera*[6], on getting the Bigi Flava[7] gig. Heard they paid you good." Rostam's leg jiggled, sending up dust from soil so dry and hard-packed it could have doubled as a discotheque floor.

5　　　Bongo means brain. Dar es Salaam is often referred to as bongoland. Bongo flava means 'Dar es Salaam flavor' and refers to the Tanzanian version of rap.

6　　　Congratulations.

7　　　Bigi is slang for big, and flava is slang for flavor.

"I did all right. You know how studio jobs go." Lucky inched his chair deeper under the thatch, out of the sun.

"Don't be modest, *braza*. It was a fresh gig. Would have snapped that one myself." Rostam played air guitar, a slight smile on his face.

Lucky coughed into his hand to hide his grimace. Even playing air guitar, the kid had sloppy form—thumb shouldn't hook over the neck like that. But then again, Rostam had snagged bigger venues lately, while he and Kim hid out at the Daladala Bar waiting for something—anything—to happen. The Bigi Flava job had been unexpected, semi-lucrative, but also brief.

"He kicked it, man," Kim said over Lucky's shoulder. "Should have heard him. *Poa kabisa*[8]. The brother can play. Anything, anytime, anywhere. That's why he's with me."

Lucky jerked. When had Kim arrived?

Rostam peered up at Kim. "Wazzup? Didn't see you there, *supa staa*[9]. We was just talkin'—"

"You ready, Lucky? Wait. I need a drink first." Kim slid into a seat and signaled a waitress across the pitch. He pretended to tip a bottle back. Subtle.

Lucky didn't want to anger the other staff, so he started to rise. Kim shook his head. "She'll get it. I'll be spending time with her later, anyhow." Kim turned to Rostam and asked, "What's that, man? A harmonica case or something?"

Rostam seemed surprised when he looked down at the box. He picked it up and held it in the palm of his hand, practically vibrating with excitement. "No. Better. It's gonna bring me luck."

Lucky eyed the little box. Not much larger than a mobile phone, it had intricate carvings worked into its surface in the style local carvers did for tourists. He squinted, trying to make out the details.

Kim reached for it, snickered. "Luck, is it? What do you have, kid? A jar full of talent in there?"

Rostam quickly pocketed the box. "Not sayin' what's inside. That's for me to know. But it'll get me everything I desire."

The young waitress appeared with Kim's beer. Kim grabbed his drink before she could set it down. He took a mouthful, favoring

---

8   Very cool.

9   Super star (slang).

her with a wink. She actually giggled. Kim had that effect on women.

As soon as the waitress left, Kim upended his Kilimanjaro and pounded it in one long gulp. He belched. "Ready?"

Rostam's leg double-timed it under the table, knocking over the empty bottles. "I was 'bout to discuss a gig with Lucky."

Kim frowned. "You sniffing petrol or something? Lucky don't need some kid to get him gigs. He's got the African Pop Orchestra and me," Kim pointed to himself, "to take care of him."

"*Aisee*[10], you guys still playin', *supa staa*?" Rostam's voice dropped to just above a whisper. "That why your guitarist waits tables at your sister's place?"

Kim jolted to his feet, an elephant about to trample a *dassie*[11]. "You—"

"*Broo*, don't." Lucky's arm darted across the table to restrain Kim. *Ai*[12], the stick of truth had a sharp point. Not many people were brave enough to point it in Kim's direction, though.

"Hey *braza*, didn't mean nothin' by it." Rostam raised both hands in a keep-the-peace gesture.

Kim shook off Lucky. "Let's go, man. Got a show to prepare for."

"I still have customers," Lucky said.

"Cleared it with my sister. You're covered."

Lucky rose. He wanted to leave before things turned ugly. What was Kim's problem? *Yesu*[13], it was going to be a long night.

"Lucky!" Rostam called after them.

Kim kept walking. Lucky slowed. "Gotta go. We'll talk later." Why would Rostam offer him a studio gig? Wouldn't he play it himself? What was the kid after?

✗ ✗ ✗ ✗

At three a.m., the African Pop Orchestra performed its last tune of the night. Kim rocked his usual *supa staa* moves at the Tiki Club

---

10   I say.

11   Also called a Hyrax. A mammal resembling a large guinea pig. Its closest living relative is the elephant.

12   An exclamation. Ah, or wow.

13   Jesus.

in Magomeni, and the ladies—the few who were present—oohed and aahed. Lucky breathed a sigh of relief when he strummed the last chord, the sudden stillness hanging in the air, almost as heavy as the smoke. Anemic clapping, laughter, and catcalls from a group of drunken older women followed the band offstage.

Kim trotted out to greet his fans—none of them a day under forty—while the Tiki Club's manager labored to intercept him. Lucky followed the manager's progress. Kim would probably sweet talk him into a couple more weeks, but Lucky knew they neared the end of the line. The Tiki Club was where musicians went to die or become irrelevant, one and the same as far as Lucky was concerned.

The manager tapped Kim's shoulder, and even from a distance, Lucky could see the news wasn't good. Kim clapped the manager on the back and probably did his verbal magic—spinning some tale or another that would get them another reprieve. Kim noticed Lucky watching him, and for a moment they locked eyes. Then Kim turned away and followed the manager through near empty bar to his office.

Time to break down his rig. He'd leave his speaker cabinets for next Sunday's show, but he needed his amp for practices. He set to work, his mood as sour as unripe mango. He and Kim had barely spoken since leaving the Daladala Bar. Ever since Lucky started working there three weeks ago, things had been tense between them. What was he supposed to do, starve?

"Got a minute?"

Lucky looked up from spooling a cord, squinted in the club's gloom. "Rostam?"

"Yah, *braza*. Caught your last set. Good stuff." Rostam cleared his throat. "I can see why you don't have no time to chase studio gigs all over the city. Thought I could help you out. I know the business, the studios, and I know who's lookin'." Rostam bounced on the balls of his feet, seemingly unable to be still.

"You stopped performing?" Lucky set down the cord and straightened.

"Yah man, I'm getting out. Too much practice, not enough pay. I got big ideas, but I'm starting small. Managing those who are worth somethin' to me. In the not too distant future you'll see 'Producer' as my tag. You grasp what I'm sayin'?"

Kim had apparently noticed Rostam and thundered their way. Great.

"What are you doing here, Rostam? Seeing how real musicians play?" Kim towered over the kid, moving so close that Rostam had to crane his neck to meet Kim's eyes.

To the kid's credit, he stood his ground. "Cool down, Kim. Just offerin' the man studio work. That's all. Not tryin' to poach anyone."

"Easy, *broo*. You know I'm not going anywhere," Lucky said. "Just hearing the kid out."

Kim crossed his arms over his chest. "Let's hear it then."

"It's an offer for Lucky only," Rostam said, taking a step backwards.

Kim puffed up, moved toward him closing the gap.

"Chill," Lucky said to Kim. Then to Rostam, he said, "Anything you say to me, you say in front of him. We don't keep secrets."

Rostam's lips thinned. He seemed to be debating something. He sidled away from Kim again. After a moment, he said, "'Kay. Here's the deal. Next Wednesday night Supa Fresh Tanzania's playing a show. You know who they is, right?"

Lucky nodded. "Yah, *broo*. The band of the moment." Good showmanship, even better bass player and singer.

"Bongo Flava," Kim said with a sneer.

Lucky ignored Kim, keeping his attention centered on Rostam. If the kid were smart, he'd do the same.

"See, they're recording another CD and need an extra guitar player for the studio," Rostam continued. He lowered his voice. "Don't know if you heard, but SFT's lead singer Marley X ain't easy to work with—likes things a certain way, you take my meanin'." Rostam paused and stared at Kim. Cleared his throat again.

"Marley X and SFT's guitarist go way back, so he ain't gonna dismiss his ass, but he wants to find a *supa staa* to lay down some complex chords for the CD. He's auditioned four or five already and said no to them all."

"You aren't auditioning?" Lucky asked.

Rostam shrugged. "Could, but probably wouldn't choose me. That's all right. Want to manage and produce, like I told you. More money in it."

"You? A producer?" Kim snickered. "That'll be the day I retire."

Swiveling toward Kim, Rostam gritted out between clenched teeth, "Then get ready, old man—"

"You ladies done arguing?" Lucky stepped between them, then turned on Kim. "You don't want to listen, fine, but I'd like to hear what he has to say." Lucky ran his hand roughly through his dreads. Did Kim have to mock the kid?

Kim opened his mouth, snapped it closed. Signaled for Rostam to continue.

"Anyhow," Rostam said, "I'm thinkin' the *braza*'s lookin' in the wrong place. Checkin' out too many young guys, not lookin' at old pros. I already told them 'bout you, Lucky. Arranged for you to come play a set, and if they like what you're offerin', I'll take a cut in what you make for the CD. Say fifty percent."

Lucky snorted. Fifty percent? The kid really was huffing petrol. "Thirty."

"Man, you stupid? Why would he pay you that much? He could probably play left-handed and still get that gig on his own," Kim added.

"Think so?" Rostam swiveled to Lucky. "Okay, thirty. This time. But you'll see. I can be useful. Wednesday night at the Peninsula. You'll be the man of the hour, and I'll be on my way to the top."

⚡   ⚡   ⚡   ⚡

The next evening, Kim rested his palms on the balcony outside Lucky's fourth floor flat, an empty beer bottle balanced on the railing. His workout clothes showed off his well-muscled arms. A towel hung from his neck.

"As much as I don't understand your interest in that *ovyo ovyo*[14] music, Supa Fresh Tanzania is big right now."

The sun had set, and lights winked on, illuminating the courtyard between the buildings. Laundry drooped from most balconies, and the smells of cooking oil, *sukuma wiki*[15], onions, and rice hung in the air.

---

14   Rubbish, garbage (slang).

15   Cooked rape leaves. A common staple food, particularly between pay periods when money is sparse. Literally means 'to push the week'.

"How can you not like Bongo Flava? It's straight up Tanzanian. Unlike what we play. Aren't you *Bwana*[16] Tanzania?" Ndombolo was exciting to play, but times and tastes had changed. Bongo Flava, the Tanzanian version of rap, had become the rage.

"Tanzanian? Rubbish. Invented by a bunch of Kenyans, I'm telling you." Kim grinned.

"Whatever you say." They'd already had this argument, and it kept leading nowhere. Why couldn't he see that they needed to shift with the times or be forgotten?

Lucky leaned against the doorway, strumming his favorite twelve-string acoustic guitar. He hummed along as his fingers glided up and down the frets coaxing a childhood gospel melody from the instrument. Bass and keyboards were cool, too, but the guitar was his first love. The way his fingers massaged the strings, the instrument's sleekness, the sounds he could make—nothing in this world like it. Only thing better was playing in front of a crowd.

Kim looked down at his empty bottle. "Agnes coming out here anytime soon, you think? A man could die of thirst."

Lucky shook his head. "Go get one yourself. She's making dinner, as you very well know."

"Really? What are we having?" He closed his eyes for a second and inhaled. "Fish in coconut milk? A man could do worse."

Lucky laughed. "You, my friend, are a scrounger. Why do I put up with you?"

"Me? Because I'm so handsome and charming, of course. And I have a great voice. And Agnes loves me. Admit it. I'm practically perfect."

"Then maybe Rostam should get you gigs, *Bwana* Perfect."

"Man, I don't need him to get me gigs. Neither do you. He's a kid. As a player he's all attitude and not much talent. What makes you think he'll be any better as a manager? Your bongoland kid manager."

Lucky stilled the guitar strings. "This is a tough town, *broo*. You make a living where you can. That a problem for you?"

And what if Kim said it would be? Kim came from a big, supportive family, but Lucky only had himself and now, Agnes. And her job didn't come close to covering their expenses.

---

16   Mister or Sir.

Kim used his gym towel to wipe his neck and face. "Just don't see why you need Rostam. He's...not right."

Before Lucky could reply, Kim added, "And why all the 'yo-wazzup-braza-street-thug-rap'?" He slouched like Rostam, crossed his arms over his chest, and struck a pose. "Heard he finished his *O-levels*[17], yo." Straightening, Kim mimicked pulling up his trousers.

Lucky didn't crack a smile, but he could feel the muscles in his face itching to do so. "I don't have to keep him on afterwards. I could—"

"And what about his *juju*[18] box story? 'It's gonna bring me luck, yo. Just look at my magic box, *braza*.' As if some box could ever turn him from zero to hero!"

"Kim—"

"Yo, I gots me a box, *braza*, cuz I can't get me no woman. My squeezebox, man. Everyday, every night, I fu—"

"Enough, broo! I get it. He's a boastful *mpumbavu*[19]. But he's also an *mpumbavu* with connections and a gig. I don't want to wait tables forever." Lucky began strumming one of the African Pop Orchestra's tunes to put an end to the discussion. It had been a hit in the late nineties and brought Kim and Lucky some renown. How fast the public moved on.

Kim looked like he was going to keep arguing, but then joined in, belting out a bawdier version of their standard, pretending his beer bottle was a microphone. The harder Lucky strummed, the louder Kim sang.

When they finished, there was laughter, applause, and even ululations made by the young ladies who lived two floors down. Kim leaned over the balcony and took a deep bow. He blew kisses to the girls, then turned back to Lucky, but didn't meet his gaze.

"I think you should sit in with SFT, man. If you haven't noticed, we're not playing as much as we used to. Be good to get your name out more."

Aisee? Did Kim just admit that?

---

17   Ordinary level. Extends from form one through form four (i.e., secondary school) that culminates with an exam leading to the National School Certificate.

18   Witchcraft, black magic.

19   Fool, arsehole.

Agnes poked her head out the doorway. She had a bit of flour on her nose, but it did nothing to dim her beauty. Six years together and she still intoxicated him with her generous hips, thick thighs, and tender smile. How had he gotten so lucky?

"Dinner's ready. Guess you can't throw that scrounger Kim out. I'll hide the beer." She shot Kim a wicked grin.

"Love you, too, sweet thing. I'd love to stay for dinner. Hope you didn't burn it this time."

She gave Kim a not-so-nice gesture that she probably learned from her work with street kids, then disappeared from the doorway.

Kim chuckled. "You going to do us all a favor and marry that girl someday?"

"You should talk, *Inspekta*[20]. How many girlfriends do you have currently?"

"Too true, my friend. But you aren't me."

Truer words had never been spoken. Lucky shouldered his guitar, motioned Kim to follow him inside. Why couldn't he admit that he was afraid to marry, to have a family? What if his children were albino? Abandonment and superstition had defined his lonely childhood. He gripped the guitar strap like a lifeline.

"You sure about the SFT gig, *broo*?"

Kim clapped him on the back. "Yeah, man. It's cool…just don't forget who your friends are."

⤬ ⤬ ⤬ ⤬

Kim and Lucky arrived at the Peninsula Club Wednesday evening. It was actually in downtown Dar, not on the peninsula, and didn't have any qualities associated with its namesake. No white beaches, no open-air tables, no palm trees. Instead, it was a dark, windowless building with neon lettering, crammed against several other bars and businesses.

Kim had driven one of his brother's 4x4s so they'd be able to carry all Lucky's gear.

They unloaded the old 4-10 speaker cabinets and carried them through the wide-mouthed alley behind the nightclub. Lucky kept his guitar case slung over his shoulder. No sense tempting thieves. He stumbled a bit as he stepped over puddles of sewage runoff,

---

20   Inspector (slang), a nosy person.

broken glass, garbage, rusting pipes, and chunks of concrete. Why had he bothered to polish his shoes?

At the back door, a uniformed guard slouched against the wall. Lucky nodded a greeting that the guard didn't return.

"Man, snap to it. This shit's heavy," Kim said, pointing to the door with his chin.

The guard slowly straightened, trudged to the door, and held it open like he'd like nothing better than to slam it in their faces.

They ignored the guard's attitude and lugged the equipment into the club.

After setup, Lucky introduced himself and Kim to the band. The lead rapper, Marley X, bumped knuckles with him.

"Heard lots about you, man. Hope you're as good as they say."

"He is, he's—"

Lucky held up his hand, and Kim went silent. Imagine that.

"I am, *broo*." Lucky pulled out his twelve-string acoustic.

"*Yesu*, you're using a Spanish guitar? You know we play Bongo Flava, right, old man?" The SFT guitarist hooted.

Lucky didn't flinch. He'd expected such a narrow-minded re-action from the guitarist. Fit his limited talent on the guitar, too. Lucky could practically feel Kim's offense on his behalf, but for-tunately Kim kept his peace.

Marley X frowned at the guitar player, then returned his atten-tion to Lucky. A slow smile spread across his face, and he nodded. "Right on, man. Like the idea. Now let's see you execute it."

They bumped knuckles again. Marley X strode toward the stage, calling over his shoulder, "Your buddy Rostam's goin' be here soon. Faida, our manager, will cue you when it's your turn. Get together with her so you know what we're doin' and how to fit in."

✗ ✗ ✗ ✗

Lucky didn't see Rostam until the show was well under way. He'd watched as Kim squeezed through the crowd on the sunken dance floor and joined a group up front near a bar. Colored lights and lasers streamed over the dancers in rhythm with the music. SFT's fans rapped along with Marley X.

Lucky relaxed backstage on a deep-set couch, resting his guitar on his lap. He strummed along to the music.

Rostam slipped in through the rear door. He paused to bum a cigarette from a stagehand, then hustled toward Lucky. He sank onto the sofa, and his leg began jiggling.

If he thought it odd Lucky held a twelve-string, he didn't mention it. "Glad you made it, Lucky. Figured you would."

Lucky slicked his dreads behind his ears. "You wanted to do this, so I'm here."

Rostam bobbed his head. "Let's get this party started."

✗   ✗   ✗   ✗

Lucky burst onto stage like he owned it. Known for his intricate finger-work, he didn't disappoint. He pulled off an impressive guitar solo, pale fingers flying over the guitar's neck. SFT's fans clapped and stomped their feet in appreciation. When the bass and drums rejoined, he led the crowd in waving their arms in the air.

During the next set break, he strode off the stage and slipped behind the heavy red curtain to loud cheers. He lived for this. Several members of Supa Fresh Tanzania—but not the guitarist—thumped him on the back, and Faida said the studio gig was his.

He was about to go find Kim when Rostam waylaid him.

"You kicked it tonight. Some of the freshest playin' I ever heard. Sincere. Just wish I had that, you know?"

"Thanks, *broo*." Lucky wiped his face with a cloth. He gently slid his guitar into its case. "You'll get your cut."

Rostam began to babble about other potential gigs.

Lucky wanted to celebrate with Kim, not stand around with Rostam. He made his excuses and shouldered the guitar case. Before he'd gone a couple of meters, Rostam caught up to him.

"Yo, Lucky, we really need to talk business. Just take a couple a minutes. I got an idea for a collaboration. You interested or what?"

"Well…"

Rostam looked so crestfallen, Lucky actually felt guilty.

A bass guitar boomed over the speakers, and several types of drums started thumping a rhythmic beat. Vibrations hummed up Lucky's legs. Marley X gave him the thumbs up as he bounced onto stage for another set.

Lucky had to shout to be heard. "Maybe. I'm pretty busy." Not true, but he didn't want to commit to anything.

"What?" Rostam held a hand to his ear. "Let's find a chill place to talk, *braza*. I think you'll be very interested in what I got to say." His eyes darted around backstage, then landed on the rear door. He mouthed, "You comin'?"

Lucky hesitated. He really wanted to find Kim, but Rostam had done him a favor. He readjusted his guitar case and followed. Better to have friends than enemies.

✗　✗　✗　✗

Lucky stood in the wide alley with Rostam, music spilling out of the club. The noise was only a little less than being inside. A single light shone from above the back door. The smell of sewage, stale beer, and garbage made Lucky's eyes water.

Rostam reached into his shirt pocket and pulled out a cigarette and matches. Striking a match on the side of an overflowing rubbish bin, he lit up and took a long drag.

The night sweltered and beads of sweat popped out on Lucky's lip. It felt like he stood under the stage lights again.

Rostam smoked in silence, pacing. Lucky shuffled his feet on the sticky pavement. Kim was waiting for him. Would he really be fine with Lucky's studio gig? They'd been friends and bandmates a long time. He didn't want to ruin that, but he needed the work. Needed to play, too.

"Thanks for comin' out here with me, Lucky." Rostam stopped pacing and peered up at Lucky, then took another drag on his cigarette. "Don't know 'bout you, but I don't plan to play forever. There are other ways to get money in this business…if you know how it's done."

"Don't know anything about that. All I know is playing," Lucky said, raising his voice to be heard over the music. He tugged on the guitar-case strap. Managers, producers, stagehands. All had their place, but…

"Fair enough, *braza*. I can respect that." He reached into his pocket and pulled out the carved box. "All I'm askin' is that you hear me out. You say 'no,' that's cool. But I think you'll see it my way. Lemme get the key. Got somethin' to show you."

Rostam felt around in his pocket until he produced the key.

Lucky waited. Nothing would change his mind. But he was curious about that box.

Rostam inserted the key into the lock, fumbled, and dropped it. The key fell by Lucky's feet.

As Lucky bent to retrieve it, his guitar case slid up his back. Something heavy smashed into the guitar and ricocheted, striking the back of his skull. He sprawled forward on the asphalt, a torrent of light bursting in his head. His guitar slipped from his shoulder as he rolled away.

A steel construction pipe smacked down where his head had just lain. He kicked out, connected with a knee, heard a grunt and something metal hitting the pavement. The box clattered to the ground, too.

"What the hell—"

Lucky sat up, scooting backwards. A fist slammed into his face, while a vicious kick to the ribs left him gasping for air. One—two—three men. They piled on him. Where had they come from?

He punched and kicked. His elbow connected with someone's nose. Blows rained down on him. They pinned him. He struggled, trying to heave them off. The pipe swung toward his head again. No chance to dodge.

Then blackness.

✗　✗　✗　✗

Lucky drifted down a tunnel, slowly moving toward light. He heard voices, but couldn't make out what they said. Arguing? Hands grabbed him, picked him up roughly. The odor of stale sweat and mothballs assaulted his nose. More harsh words. He hit the pavement. Then pain. Excruciating.

His eyes flew open. He tried to scream, but something was stuffed in his mouth. Two men argued with Rostam. One wore a Tupac T-shirt and gripped a machete with blood on the blade. The guy's hands shook, and blood dripped from his nose. Must be the one Lucky nailed.

"You *mpumbavu*. Can't you even cut straight?" Rostam said. "I wanted all the fingers, not a finger and a couple of little pieces."

"Sorry, man, he's new. His first time. You want me to cut off the rest?" the other guy said. He wore a Peninsula guard's uniform.

"I want the other hand. All the fingers, Gosbert."

"No can do. We need one hand whole. Will bring more that way. Unless you don't want your million shillings?" The one called Gosbert crossed his arms over his chest.

Still dazed, Lucky looked at his hand. He tried to scream again and roll away, but his arms and legs wouldn't cooperate.

"Shit, the *mzungu*'s awake. Stop him," Gosbert said. He bared his teeth, a big gap prominent.

Lucky stilled when the wicked-looking machete blade was thrust under his chin. Tupac guy's hands still shook, the knife nicking Lucky's neck. A tear rolled down Lucky's cheek, and he clutched his wounded hand to his chest. Blood quickly soaked his shirt, the sharp metallic scent filling his nostrils. The pinky was completely gone. The ring and middle fingers sliced off before the first knuckle. *Yesu*, why would they do this?

Rostam squatted next to Lucky, bouncing on the balls of his feet. He scooped the box from the pavement, flipped open the lid without using the key, and snatched up a severed finger. He dropped it into the box. "Perfect fit, no? Told you it would gimme a bit of luck." He added the other two finger pieces, snapped the lid closed, and pocketed the box.

Lucky tried to speak, but when he went to pull out the gag, Tupac shook his head and pressed the knife harder against his neck.

Rostam smiled. "Surprised? Like I said, Lucky, there are other ways to make money if a man has brains enough."

Then it hit him. They were going to sell his body parts. Albinos brought a premium in the witchcraft trade to the Congo.

But this was Dar es Salaam, not a backwards border village. People didn't just kill one another without consequences. Lucky scanned the alley wildly.

"Lookin' for help?" Rostam chuckled and bent over Lucky. "Haven't you figured it out yet, *braza*? Your buddy Kim is in on this. You're worth more to him dead than you ever was alive. Your leg alone will buy him an ocean of beer."

Lucky lashed out at Rostam with his elbow, hitting him squarely in the chest. The blow dumped him on his arse. Gosbert and Tupac chortled.

Kim a betrayer? Never.

Lucky started to roll so he could continue his attack. The knife's blade sliced deeper into his skin.

"Cool down," Tupac said.

Lucky stilled.

Rostam pushed himself up and dusted himself off, his jeans blackened from the pavement. Before Lucky could react, Rostam smashed the steel pipe on Lucky's ankle.

Lucky screamed in a way he never imagined he could. He cursed and rolled to the side.

"Enough, Rostam. Time is running out." Gosbert pointed at Tupac. "Give me the knife, and I'll do it now."

"Wait, that's not the deal. You need to take him somewhere. Too many people have seen us together." Rostam wheeled on Gosbert.

"Not enough time. I say we do it and go."

"No, you need to take him away." Rostam pulled on Lucky's legs. "Here, I'll help you dump him in the boot. You parked down there?"

Gosbert sighed, then turned to Lucky. "You better be worth this." He grabbed Lucky under the arms and lifted.

Lucky struggled. He couldn't let them take him away. No one would know what happened. Tupac pointed the knife at Lucky, but he ignored it.

Do or die.

He kicked and flailed with all his strength. He sent Rostam stumbling backwards, and forced Gosbert to drop him on the ground. He yanked the gag from his mouth, taking deep gulps of air, and screamed.

Gosbert bent over Lucky and grabbed his dreadlocks. He used them to slam Lucky's head into the pavement, cutting off his cry.

Lucky fought unconsciousness. He grabbed Gosbert's arm with his good hand, pulled it to him, and latched on with his teeth. Gosbert cursed and let go of Lucky's hair. Rostam charged Lucky with the construction pipe again. This time Lucky was ready. He waited until Rostam was almost on top of him, then kicked Rostam as hard as he could in the groin. Rostam dropped like a stone.

"Kill him!" Gosbert screamed, still trying to dislodge Lucky from his arm. He pounded on Lucky with his other fist.

Tupac stood motionless, the machete in hand.

"Kill him!" Gosbert screamed again.

Lucky could feel himself slipping away. His ears ringing from Gosbert's blows, his fight waning. He tasted Gosbert's blood and hung on.

Tupac moved toward Lucky and raised the knife. Lucky wouldn't have a chance to avoid the strike.

A loud crack. Glass shards hit Lucky's face. Tupac stumbled and went down, the blade clattering on the pavement. What was happening?

Another crack. More glass showered him, and something sticky spattered his skin and hair. Gosbert tumbled on top of him. He shoved at Gosbert, who lay unmoving.

He was free.

He rolled, then lurched, trying to rise. He fell to his knees, his ankle on fire, unable to hold weight. Blood streamed from his hand, the pain immense.

"You sick fuckers! I'll kill you." Kim charged past and lunged at Tupac, who had staggered to his feet.

Relief flooded Lucky's system like a drug.

Kim wielded two jagged stumps that had once been beer bottles. He slashed at Tupac, who was losing a lot of blood but couldn't retreat without Kim stabbing him in the back. Gosbert lay on the ground moaning. Where was Rostam?

"Kim, look out!"

Rostam charged Kim from the side. He swung his pipe, aiming for Kim's skull. Kim threw himself to the side, but the pipe connected with his temple, and he went down.

The knife. Where was it? Lucky looked around frantically, saw it glint, and crawled to it. He scooped it up in his uninjured hand. He held the machete awkwardly and scrabbled toward Rostam.

"Rostam!" Lucky croaked. "You and me."

Rostam spun away as Lucky slashed the machete with as much power as he possessed. A bright line of red popped up on Rostam's thigh. The pipe dropped with a loud clank, and Rostam collapsed on the pavement, screaming.

Lucky turned. Gosbert supported Tupac as they limped down the alley to their car, leaving a trail of blood. He debated going after them, but scrambled toward Kim, wanting to make sure his friend was okay. Kim moaned and opened his eyes.

"Did I get them?" His words were slurred.

Lucky nodded.

"Yeah, you sure did." He clasped Kim's shoulder. "Thanks."

Kim sat up, gripped his head, his blue eyes unfocused. "Man, was that Rostam? Got a bad headache. Need a beer. Seem to have lost mine."

"Easy, *broo*. Just relax. Think you got concussed." He probably had, too, but felt surprisingly clear-headed.

From the corner of his eye, Lucky saw a blur. Legs uncoordinated, arms flailing, Rostam made a wild run for the parking lot. A few meters from the alley's mouth, he stumbled and disappeared. A splash. Lucky rose and limped after him. Rostam lay twitching in a puddle of sewage water, facedown. Lucky rolled him over. Rostam's skin was grey and almost as light as Lucky's. He'd cut Rostam down to the bone, could see it exposed. What little blood he seemed to have left quickly pulsed out.

For a moment, Lucky remained frozen like Tupac guy. Was he a murderer, too?

He hobbled back down the alley and picked up the old T-shirt they'd used to gag him. Holding it with his teeth, he tore it into a large strip and tied it around Rostam's thigh. For once Rostam stayed still. Blood slicked Lucky's hand, but he finally got the bandage tight. The rest was up to God.

✗　✗　✗　✗

Lucky scrubbed his bandaged hand across his nose in a futile attempt to block the fear, urine, and ammonia smell peculiar to hospitals. He glanced at the clock in the hallway. Already lunchtime, and he still sat on a bench waiting for Kim. What was taking so long? Stitches dotted Lucky's face where glass shards had sliced him, and plaster of paris encased his ankle and calf. The overhead flickering bulb aggravated his splitting headache, and he had more bruises than he could count. Kim had taken a single blow to the head. Could it have been worse than he realized?

A door opened down the hall, and Kim emerged with a sizable bandage on his temple. He rapped gently on his forehead.

"Thick as steel, my friend." He came and sat next to Lucky, leaned against the dingy wall that showed the faint imprint of bodies. "How you doing, man?" Kim nudged Lucky with his shoulder.

Lucky sagged, seeming to collapse into himself. "You were right about the kid. I just saw opportunity. He played me just right." He wanted to scream or smash things—anything to make it better—but just felt numb. Maybe the drugs the doctors had given him?

Kim started to say something, but Lucky raised his bandaged hand. "Don't. I just need to go home. Agnes will come from the dispensary soon. Doctor said I had to take antibiotics. Make sure I don't get an infection."

Kim glanced at the bandage, only Lucky's thumb and pointer finger intact, then quickly averted his gaze. They sat, listening to the clack of heels as hospital staff and patients walked up and down the hallway.

Kim shifted his weight on the bench.

"Rostam's dead," he said. "Police couldn't get the *PF3*[21] filled out in time. Not that it would have much mattered, too much blood lost before you bandaged him."

"Fucking police," Lucky said. So Rostam was dead? How would he feel about being a murderer once the medicines wore off? Getting chopped into pieces and almost sold by traffickers had a way of soothing one's conscience. Pissed him off Rostam came out a hero.

Kim nodded like he could read Lucky's mind. "Got better than he deserved. At least they'll look for those guys for murder now."

They'd told the police that Rostam fell victim to the albino traffickers. Kept Lucky from being arrested. The police weren't likely to care about the truth—just lining their pockets. And Lucky didn't have the kind of money to pay the endless rounds of bribes needed to beat a murder rap.

---

21   Police Form 3. A form that must be filled out by the police after a serious injury before a doctor can legally treat the patient. Many relatively minor injuries have lead to death because a patient would not be admitted to the hospital for treatment until the paperwork was filed with the police. The PF3 is currently being revised so that victims in cases involving gender-based violence and/or serious injury will be able to seek treatment first and then follow up with the PF3 afterwards.

He reached around on his other side and opened his guitar case. He pulled out Rostam's box. "Docs didn't even try to reattach. Too long at the police station."

"I'm sorry. I wish—"

"Don't sweat it, *broo*. You saved the rest of me."

"What are you going to do with the box?"

"You want it? Might bring you luck. I hear we albinos do that." He laughed, his voice on the edge of hysteria. "You can sell my fingers. Bring you a good price."

"Man, stop it. That's sick."

Lucky shrugged. He opened the box and examined his bloodless fingers, like little gravestones lined up in a row. Hard to believe only hours before they'd strummed a guitar. He could almost feel the memory. He'd never do that again. Maybe they should have killed him. He snapped the lid closed. The sound echoed off the concrete corridor. "Music was all I had."

"That's not true—"

"It is! Don't get it, do you? *Supa staa* Kim. Lead singer. Ladies' man. Funny guy. Me? My whole life I've been the *mzungu* who could play guitar. When we were on top, I was finally the guitarist who happened to be albino." Lucky pounded his fist on his leg. "Now, I'm just…"

He heaved himself up, then hobbled over to a waste bin and threw the box away. "No more luck for old Lucky."

"You can get your luck back, man." Kim spoke so quietly that Lucky almost missed it.

Hope rose in his chest, and he hated himself for it. He stared at the waste bin. "It's over," he whispered, then with more force, "It's over."

Kim walked to the bin, plucked out the box. "We'll see about that, my friend."

✗　✗　✗　✗

Lucky shifted nervously backstage, his ankle still a little sore. Five months had passed since his "accident." Was he really ready to play in public?

Kim had surprised him by having both his acoustic and electric guitars retooled for a lefty. Lucky, who could play anything musical, had found himself a novice again. He almost quit in despair, but Kim hadn't let him, urging him to practice day and night.

His thumb absently traced the stumps that had once been his fingers. His right-handed fingering wasn't perfect, but he could play. That was something.

The music community had rallied around him, and he'd become a minor celebrity again, even doing an advertisement against albino killings. Inundated with invitations to record and jam, Lucky chafed at his albino-who-lived fame, but he wasn't about to let the opportunity to play slip away. Even if tonight's show honored Rostam's memory. He grimaced.

Kim, the unsung hero in all of this, didn't seem to mind. He stood next to Lucky, unconsciously bobbing his head to the music. Lucky smiled. He would get Kim to appreciate Bongo Flava yet.

After the song ended, Supa Fresh Tanzania's guitarist exited the stage and jogged toward Lucky.

"Man, you're on." The guitarist clapped him on the back like they were old friends.

Lucky reached into his pocket and pulled out the box. He stared at it a moment, lost in the memory.

"We all miss him," the guitar player said. "Cool you have something to remember him by."

"Yah, *broo*. I think of him everyday." Lucky flipped the box open. Selecting a guitar pick, he snapped the lid closed, and tossed it to Kim. He held the pick between forefinger and thumb. He'd get used to it eventually. He ran onto the stage amid Marley X's introduction and cheers from the audience.

Maybe he still had a little luck left.

MY LIVING IS DYING

by Laird Long

Captain fired three times at Dutchboy Solito. Solito's body did a little jig like Hitler in Paris and then smashed through the breakfast table and bounced off the dirty hardwood floor. The body twitched and then noodled.

The girl didn't move her chair. She had a spoon in her hand, but now there was nothing to eat, except lead. She was beautiful—in a dark alley kind of way. Not so beautiful in the harsh reality of morning. Her bathrobe hung loose on her skinny body, an open invitation to anyone. She was whimpering.

Captain turned to face her. The gun turned with him. They both foresaw the coming of death.

"P-please, Mister," the girl pleaded. "I ain't done nothin'." Tears were marking twisted trails down her harsh white face.

Captain spoke with precision and economy, his expression as hard and blank as a granite tombstone. "Dutchboy was skimming. Running whores—like you. He should've known Callaghan wouldn't like that."

The girl didn't bother looking at Captain's face. There was nothing there for her. She looked at the gaping maw of his gun. She slowly and shakily stood up. She untied her bathrobe. It slid to the floor quietly, coiled around her feet like a snake. She was naked. Her body was hollow and empty; a place where dreams turned ugly.

"See anythin' you like?" she asked, trying to sound bold, but coming off scared. "W-why don't we have a little fun, Mister?"

"I'm here on business," Captain replied matter-of-factly. He squeezed the trigger and the gun barked a command that the girl had no choice but to obey. The bullet tore a bloody path through her left breast and buried in her heart. Her body eased down the blood-spattered wall like a tire flattening.

Captain strode over to the pair on the floor. The girl's chest heaved slightly, something rattled in her throat. He put the gun to the back of her head and fired off a round. The Service had taught him: always check for survivors.

✗　✗　✗　✗

Two weeks later, Hunky Callaghan was sitting behind the big, polished oak desk in his downtown office, as usual. Guitar Wyman was seated in a chair in front of the desk, rolling a cigarette with the care and concentration of a musician tuning his instrument.

Callaghan was a big man, with sandy blond hair, a heavy face, and tortoise-shell glasses. He was dressed in a flamboyant purple suit and blue tie. Seated behind the huge desk, he looked like a movie mogul contemplating his next epic. And he had the manners to fit the role. Wyman, on the other hand, was short and skinny, with a pained face and an ulcerated gut. He was practically bald.

"Hunk, I'm tellin' ya, that guy's dangerous," Wyman whined.

"Of course he's dangerous, that's why he's working for me. I'm not running a tea cozy factory here. Besides, better working fer me, than agin me."

"I'll go along with ya there. But I still think the guy's a nut case. Shell-shocked outta his gourd."

"Captain is a war hero," Hunky replied with heavy dignity. "He was with the British Army for the entire campaign—six long years. He was wounded five times and has a chestful of medals."

"Yeah, and it's two years later and the war's still goin' on in what's left of his mind."

"Ah, Guitar, that's where you and I differ. I understand and therefore can use a man like Captain, while you merely fear him. He saw a lot of horrific things during the war, no doubt, killed a lot of men. For him, you're partially right, the killing hasn't stopped. Yet. One day, though, the death and destruction will come to an end."

"Maybe after you're dead," Wyman cracked. He jerked the cigarette out of his mouth and exhaled a cloud of poisonous gas. "Or maybe, just maybe, he becomes one of them born-again do-gooders and turns you in."

Callaghan smiled complacently. He sought to educate. "Again, you are letting fear cloud your judgment. With a man like Captain, one day he will simply have had enough of killing. Do you know what he'll do then?"

"Yeah, open a posie shop," Wyman replied, "and send a few to your grave." He smiled a twisted smile.

"He'll just walk away. He'll be suddenly sickened by what he has done, and he'll want to get as far away from the killing as possible. We'll never see Captain again, when that time comes." Callaghan leaned back in his chair and nodded to himself in agreement. His jowls nodded back.

Wyman almost jumped out of his oily hide when there was a loud knock on the office door.

"Come in," Callaghan called out confidently.

Captain walked into the room. He was a tall, thin man, with coal-black hair and a small, neat mustache. His posture was ramrod straight, and his clothing was clean and severe. He was a man who didn't make messes—he cleaned them up.

"Ah, back from the front, Captain," Callaghan grinned. "It's been awhile."

Wyman shrank down into his green leather chair and patted his jacket pocket, feeling the hard, reassuring shape of a gun.

"Mission completed, Callaghan," Captain said. His eyes were as black as his hair—two bottomless pools drained of all feeling.

"Good, good," Callaghan cooed. He rubbed his fat hands together. "I believe this is yours, then." He opened a desk drawer, pulled out an envelope, and carelessly tossed it on the desk.

Captain picked it up, opened it, and carefully counted the fifty one hundred dollar bills.

"Can we get a receipt?" Wyman joked, from deep within the bowels of his chair.

Callaghan spoke: "Captain, I hate to put you back into action right away, but I have a problem. A reporter, Jersey Johnson, is trying to make a name for himself by doodling in my affairs. He does the crime beat for the *Post*, and I'm frankly getting sick and tired of reading about my business every day. Also, he's getting a little too close to the truth. Do you understand what I'm saying?"

"I understand that I've got some business to attend to," Captain responded.

"Yes, business." Callaghan nodded sagely. "The sooner the better," he added.

Wyman screwed up enough courage to ask a question: "Hey Captain, is everythin' business to you, or do you ever make anythin' personal?"

Captain looked at Wyman for a long time. Wyman squirmed under the harsh glare, and even Callaghan started to sweat a cold sweat as silence squeezed tension into the room.

"I've never had reason to," Captain replied finally. "Until now." He wheeled around and left the room.

Wyman patted his gun pocket. Callaghan stared at the dark, empty doorway.

✗   ✗   ✗   ✗

A man stumbled out of the revolving door of the *Post* building and stopped on the sidewalk to turn up his coat collar. The wind was howling, and the cold was made even more bitter by the time: three a.m. The man hunched his shoulders and ran for his car. A second man stepped from behind a lamp post in the parking lot and stopped the running man dead in his tracks.

"We're going for a walk," Captain said quietly. He stepped into the light and the other man gasped in surprise.

"Dennis," he said. Then he saw the big, Army-issue gun. "What's the meaning of this?"

"Walk," Captain ordered.

Jersey Johnson recognized the futility, and danger, in arguing. He turned around and the pair headed for a narrow, unlit alley that ran off the empty parking lot. They stopped at the mouth of the alley.

"Turn around," Captain said.

Johnson turned slowly. He swallowed hard. "We thought you were dead, Dennis. After two years, we thought you were dead." Johnson stretched his gloved hands out in a pleading gesture. The cold wind whistled around the corner and slapped against his face.

"Aren't you even going to ask how your wife and kids are doing?" Johnson asked, frantic now. "Don't you even care? You haven't seen or talked to them in eight years! Do you even care that I'm living with them!?" Johnson screamed. The wind caught his words and blew them away. He struggled to regain his composure. "I'm sorry," he said, and began to cry.

Captain stared long and hard at the sobbing man. "Don't be sorry," he said. "I'm here on business. Nothing personal."

The big gun roared twice and Johnson stumbled backwards into the alley. He was swallowed by the blackness.

Captain took a last look at the empty space that had been a man and then turned around and headed uptown—for Hunky Callaghan's office, thirty blocks away.

✗   ✗   ✗   ✗

What did you say!?" Callaghan yelled.

Wyman was shaking like a tree caught in a Kansas twister. "I–I said that Jersey Johnson is, I mean was, Captain's brother."

Suddenly, a shotgun blast exploded somewhere downstairs. Then another. Wyman and Callaghan stared at each other wild-eyed.

Fear held them silent, until Callaghan finally spoke, in a whisper: "Well, um, how do you know for—"

"Fischer just told me that the cops found Johnson's body in an alley. A cop on our bill told Fischer that they found a picture of a man in uniform in Johnson's wallet—someone Fischer might know. There was writin' on the back of the picture: 'To my brother, I'll be back when it's over, over here!' The cop said the man in the picture was Captain."

Callaghan pulled a huge handkerchief from his suit pocket and swabbed his humid forehead. Three shots rang out in rapid succession. The explosions were louder now. Closer!

"What are we gonna do?" Wyman screamed, terror crawling up and down his bony face.

"I–I, why did he kill his own brother? He, um, could have told me," Callaghan stumbled, trying to get his wild thoughts in order. "It, um, doesn't make sense. Uh, it doesn't add up. I—"

A shotgun blasted twice more, someone screamed in the pain of death. This time the noise was deafening. The war was just outside the office door.

"We, uh, should—"

The door was shattered by a shotgun blast. Captain kicked the splintered door off its hinges and advanced into the room. He tossed the smoking shotgun aside and pulled a Colt .45 out of a side holster. Wyman fumbled to get his own gun out of his pocket, but his shaking hand was slick with sweat. Captain caught the movement and fired twice. Two red holes popped open on Wyman's face and started leaking life. He fell sideways, a dumb expression on his face, and hit the floor. He left the world the same way he entered.

Callaghan shoved his fat hands into the air. "I surrender, Captain!" he screamed.

Captain pointed the gun at Callaghan's big belly. A belly fed by crime.

"Mission completed, Callaghan," Captain said.

"W-why d-did you do it? Why didn't you tell me?" Callaghan wailed. His glasses fogged over.

"It was business," Captain replied flatly.

"Then w-what's all this?" Callaghan complained shrilly, jabbing a quivering finger at the death and destruction littering his once-elegant office.

"Business," Captain said. He fired the gun four times in rapid succession, opening up Callaghan's chest. Hot blood splashed onto Captain's clean suit as Callaghan toppled over his desk and smashed into the wall. "Family business," Captain said quietly. Callaghan fell into a forever sleep.

⚔   ⚔   ⚔   ⚔

Captain slowly walked back through the smoke-filled ruins of Callaghan's offices. He stopped to glance out a broken window, at the police cars massed outside. Their flashing red lights chopped up the darkness like flares. He stepped over two blasted bodies at the door of the building and walked out into the cold, early morning gloom.

"Put your hands over your head!" a policeman yelled. "Now!"

The scatter-guns and handguns of twenty policemen targeted Captain as he stepped out of the wreckage.

"War's over," Captain said to himself as he slowly raised his weapon. A volley of gunfire saluted his death.

Long pounds out fiction in all genres. Big guy, sense of humor. Writing credits include: *Blue Murder Magazine*, *Plots With Guns*, *Hardboiled*, *Thriller UK*, *Damnation Books*, *Bullet*, *Robot*, *Eternal Night*, *Another Realm*, *The Dark Krypt*, *Baen's Universe*, and stories in the anthologies

Darkways of the Wizard, Your Darkest Dreamspell, The Mammoth Book of New Comic Fantasy, The Mammoth Book of Jacobean Whodunits, and The Mammoth Book of Perfect Crimes and Impossible Mysteries.

LONG-LOST 1916 SHERLOCK HOLMES FILM FOUND!

Cinémathèque Française announced that a negative of "Sherlock Holmes," featuring William Gillette's groundbreaking role as the great detective, was recently discovered. The plot of the film draws on several stories from the Canon, but is Gillette's original interpretation.

The film is being restored in partnership with the San Francisco Silent Film Festival. The European premiere will take place in January 2015, and the San Francisco Silent Film festival will host the American premiere in May 2015. We are looking forward to watching the film, hopefully in the company of other admirers of Holmes and Gillette.

THE ADVENTURE OF THE EMPTY LIGHTHOUSE

by Jack Grochot

I had just returned from a brisk stroll to the Great Peter Street post office when our landlady, Mrs Hudson, stopped me at the bottom of the stairs to inform me my fellow-lodger, Sherlock Holmes, was entertaining a comely young female in our flat on this perfectly pleasant afternoon in the summer of 1897. "The door and the windows are open to circulate the fine breeze," Mrs Hudson went on, "and I can hear them giggling all the way down here. She gave her name as Miss Penelope Cartier when I showed her up, and she addressed him as 'my darling Sherlock' as she went across the threshold. I don't think she is a client; rather, a sweetheart. Oh, this is so exciting, Dr Watson!"

"This is all news to me," I reacted in astonishment. "He didn't say he was expecting a visitor, and I certainly am unaware of any romantic involvement he might be pursuing."

Curious and perplexed, I ascended the steps two at a time, only to find when I reached the top that Holmes was escorting the attractive brunette to the doorway, his bony hand draped over her forearm, and a warm smile on both their faces.

"Halloa, Watson, you are just in time to exchange how-do-you-dos with my secret agent in South London," he revealed, "who has come to relate to me a humourous encounter with my prime suspect in the Brixton jewel heist." Holmes introduced us and walked Miss Cartier down to the front door, maneuvering with her at his side onto the stoop to hail a cab that would take her to the Underground station.

Whistling, he emerged once again at the second-floor entrance to our diggings, saying Miss Cartier was a lovely and charming individual. "But in her line of work, those two attributes are essential."

"What does she do?" I inquired.

"She earns her living in the bedroom of a bawdy house at Lambeth," came his shocking reply. "I first questioned her during the investigation of a case you exploited in a magazine article, titled 'The Deadly Goodge Street Affair.' She furnished valuable data that helped lead to the solution."

"Mrs Hudson will be disappointed to learn you are not Miss Cartier's suitor," I suggested. "Our landlady thinks you two are a giddy couple."

"Not my type," Holmes countered. "It would be too difficult a challenge to make an honest woman out of her. Now instruct me, Watson, on your recollection of the environment in Cornwall—you traveled there, I recall, on holiday with your late wife."

"Ah, yes, what a joyous week we spent together," I remembered, digressing into a melancholy reverie. "'John!' she shouted. 'Step away from the edge!' Oblivious, I peered into the precipice on the seashore, watching the violent waves crash against the jagged wall. 'This turbulent wind could make me a widow,' Mary whined. 'I can't bear the thought of life without you, my love.'"

"Snap out of it, my good friend, and describe the surroundings," Holmes broke in. "Did you chance upon the Wolf Rock lighthouse?"

"Of course," I mentioned as I recovered. "The gusts and gales mimic the cry of a wolf and the rock is in the shape of its head. It is situated at the mouth of the English Channel, almost exactly halfway between the Lizard and Scilly isles. It is a treacherous navigational hazard. The lighthouse was constructed over a nine-year period because of the inclement weather conditions. It is made of granite to withstand the pounding of the wicked surf."

"It is to Cornwall we must go on the eight o'clock train tomorrow morning," Holmes disclosed. "A tantalising mystery there beckons me."

"A mystery, you say?" I queried. "What are the circumstances?"

"Skullduggery, no doubt. It seems that lighthouse keepers are disappearing in succession, three at last count, the chief keeper and his two assistants," Holmes continued, stroking his pointy chin and moaning to lend an ominous tone to the situation.

"The trio shared a cottage and a barn, which have been found abandoned, along with the horses and other livestock. The letter I received yesterday from the chairman of the lighthouse commission painted a bleak picture of the conditions, not the least of which is the darkened beacon. A shipwreck is inevitable if the police or I fail to restore the operation back to normal. The chairman is trying to round up volunteers to man the lamp, clean and polish the lens, and maintain a supply of oil for the flame. But a contingent of volunteers cannot carry on indefinitely. Besides, there exists a shortage of willing villagers, because many believe the absence of the regular crew is due to a supernatural event."

"You mean a poltergeist?" I wondered, to which Holmes responded:

"Yes, the mischievous spirit of a worker who fell to his death from the pinnacle while setting in place one of the granite slabs."

"I can't imagine, in this enlightened day and age, that someone would attach credence to such malarkey," I marveled. "How backward some people must be."

"Nonetheless, that is what the chairman is up against. His task is daunting," Holmes commented. "We shall see what we can do to dispel the superstitions of the faint-hearted. In the meantime, Watson, what say we dine early today at Luigi's and ride from there to the Old Imperial Theatre for an evening performance of 'A Bungled Arrangement' that the *Times* critic raved about in this morning's edition?"

"An excellent proposal. I'm in the mood for pasta and a musical comedy," I concurred.

The supper was delightful, the play hilarious, and our trip back to Baker Street uneventful, except for the hansom driver's foul language when an inebriated passenger in the vehicle attempted to alight without paying his fare as we climbed aboard at the theatre.

Just after sunrise the next day, we packed our carry-alls and made our way to Paddington station for the nine-hour eastbound rail journey to Cornwall, with stops at a dozen or more towns, including one in Newton Abbot on the River Teign to take on more water, and Plymouth, where we uncoupled from two coaches.

As we arrived at our destination at Land's End in western Cornwall, Sherlock Holmes bounded onto the depot platform and breathed in the salty air, remarking that when he retired, it would be to a place near the ocean. "It is stimulating, to be sure," he added wistfully.

Holmes surveyed the undulating landscape, taking long drags on his cherry-wood pipe, while I reminisced about the days and nights I enjoyed with Mary in guest houses at Penzance, Helston, and Falmouth, each a quaint Cornish historical attraction.

Soon after we disembarked, a small, grizzled chap, wearing a plaid flannel shirt, knit hat, and denim overalls held up by red suspenders, greeted us with a firm handshake, announcing himself as the chairman of the lighthouse commission, Oscar Winchell. He was armed with a double-barrel shotgun at his side in his left hand.

"I read the wire you sent me today from Paddington station, Mr Holmes," he began, "so I knew when to expect you. Probably you're both famished. My little missus has cooked a beef stew for all of us, and after we eat I can show you to your quarters—I'm putting you up in the lighthouse keepers' cottage. They won't be needing it anytime soon. With a good night's rest, you can start your investigation first thing in the morning. The authorities have failed thus far, and they have all but given up finding our missing men."

"Is there an inn nearby that caters to foreigners?" Holmes wanted to know.

"Why, yes, the Hideaway Tavern has rooms for rent on the second floor, and there are always nefarious characters from around the world staying there," Winchell advised.

"That is where I shall commence the search for your lighthouse crew tomorrow," Holmes contended.

"If and when you locate Charlie Neff and his helpers, it'll be none too soon," the worried gent grumbled, "because the flame on Wolf Rock is extinguished. I have exhausted my list of volunteers, and not one of them wants to do the chores twice. I did them myself the last two nights, and was awake half the day doing maintenance. I need sleep, or my health will fail for certain. I fear a vessel will smash aground tonight, or the next night, or in the near future unless the beacon goes back into operation quickly."

"It is your good fortune that you did not vanish as well," Holmes told the chairman.

"That's the reason I take ole Betsy along wherever I go," Winchell answered, raising his weapon onto his shoulder and patting the butt proudly. "I expect you two came prepared for a fight also?"

Holmes winked and I nodded, then we climbed aboard Winchell's wagon for the trip over several grassy hills to his home.

While driving his team, the commissioner turned in the seat toward Holmes and asked pointedly: "What is your interest in foreigners? Do you suppose some sort of international plot has been brewing?"

"I have a theory, but it is far too early to discuss it. I need more data before I make a deduction," Holmes cryptically stated. "Is your wife a good cook?"

"A wonderful one—that's why I'm so pudgy," Winchell replied. "She satisfies my hearty appetite. You'll drool over her breakfasts, too. She'll say you could do with more meat on your frame, Mr Holmes. As for you, Dr Watson, you'll not shed even one gram if you're here any length of time. But let's hope our predicament is resolved in a flash. I pity the poor seamen whose ship breaks apart on Wolf Rock. And here we are, home, sweet home. I'll put the Belgians up and feed them, then I'll join you in the dining room."

Mrs Winchell, a head taller than her husband, approached the front gate and invited us inside for a glass of sparkling wine, made from Regent grapes grown locally. "Oscar always partakes of his favourite red before he sits at the table for his evening meal," she allowed. "I'm not against it, because I always imbibe a wee bit with him."

The conversation at supper was dominated by chitchat about the inhabitants of the village and farms around it, facts that Holmes stored in his brain attic, as he referred to his memory for tiny details. He listened intently to the Winchells, interrogated them about ne'er-do-wells in the vicinity, and awed them with the particulars of missing persons cases in which he had been requested by Scotland Yard to intervene.

Afterward, Holmes was even more eager to visit the Hideaway Tavern because of something said by Oscar Winchell, an off-hand reference to the innkeeper, Eddie McKeeta, whom Winchell described as a sympathiser with rebel elements of a movement in Northern Ireland to secede from British rule.

In the parlour, while Mrs Winchell was busy in the kitchen with the dishes, Holmes suggested the commission chairman drive us to the cottage where we would stay and then join us for a pint of ale at McKeeta's pub.

"My better half disapproves of my patronising the establishment—it's a den of iniquity—but I guess she won't mind if I am accompanying you on official business," Winchell postulated to accept Holmes's proposal.

We took our carry-alls to the barn and set them in the wagon while Winchell hitched his team, then we rode to the lighthouse keepers' cottage about a kilometer away. Holmes peppered our host with queries concerning the clientele at the inn, the duties of the lighthouse keepers, their habits, and the circumstances surrounding their disappearances.

The sun had dropped below the horizon by the time we arrived at the cottage, and Winchell showed us inside in the dim light of dusk. "It gives me the heebie-jeebies when I come here to check on things in the dark," he admitted, "even with my Betsy."

As he ushered us through the unlocked door of the cottage, Winchell commented that his wife had tidied up the place and changed the linen the day before, so we would be sure to feel comfortable.

"That was considerate, but unfortunate," Holmes complained, "because I might have discovered some clue as to whether the men were abducted here or at Wolf Rock."

"It was definitely at the lighthouse, or on the way to it," Winchell asserted. "The night Charlie Neff went missing, the other two told me he had left this area under his own power, on foot and on schedule—normal as could be."

"Then I deduce there is only one probability of their whereabouts now," Holmes speculated, but he did not elaborate. "Shall we see what Mr McKeeta and his cohorts at the Hideaway Tavern are up to?"

Puzzled by Holmes's speculation, Winchell returned to the wagon, mumbling to himself, and, with the reins, he guided the pair of sorrel horses in the direction of the village, with me seated next to him on the left and Holmes, silent, at his right side.

The entrance to the inn was wide open, the door propped against the stone wall with a mop handle. We found an empty table in the centre of the large, smoky room, which had sawdust on the floor plus walls decorated with Medieval weapons and armour. It was occupied by a dozen or so boisterous male customers who grew quiet as we sat. A waitress with shoulder-length, stringy black hair took our order and quickly brought three mugs of ale that were poured from kegs by a tall, stout fellow with a shock of curly red hair protruding from underneath a derby. "That's Eddie McKeeta behind the bar," Winchell informed us, "and the woman who brought our drinks is his concubine, Millie. She'll strike up a conversation at our table to find out who you are and what two well-dressed strangers are doing in this neck of the woods.

"Over there, standing in the corner with their heads together, are two ex-convicts, Malcolm Ingram and Joe Gratta—they did a ten-year stretch in Harmarville Penitentiary for kidnapping a child and extorting a five thousand pound ransom from her parents. They're a couple of felons I think would be capable of anything illegal."

"What would they gain by absconding with your lighthouse keepers?" Holmes wondered.

"No telling," Winchell answered. "They could have done it just out of ugliness."

"Did the police question them?" Holmes went on.

"The police haven't confided in me what they have accomplished," Winchell replied. "To be honest, they're not intellectual or ambitious, and I don't think they have made much progress, other than to write a few notes."

"I'll talk to the official in charge of the investigation and see what direction it has taken," Holmes promised. "Is there anyone else in here who merits my scrutiny?"

"This place is crawling with suspects," Winchell professed. "There's Skinny Harris at the bar, in the striped shirt and goatee— he's a crooked gambler and a friend of most criminals, mixed up in all sorts of shady dealings. Then, three tables away behind you, drinking with a group of miscreants, is Ravi Kolli, a thief who served time in Harmarville for his daylight burglaries. And then we have the gang at the billiard table, robbers and cutthroats all. See why my dear wife forbids me to come here?"

Winchell was on the mark about Millie. When she came over casually to ask if we wanted more ale, she prodded Winchell to introduce us to her. "You gentlemen on holiday from the city?" she pried.

"Not exactly," Holmes spoke up. "We've come to solve a riddle."

"A riddle? What riddle?" she enquired.

"How is an empty lighthouse like an abandoned bee hive?" Holmes answered cryptically.

"Ya got me, mister. How?" Millie chuckled.

"They both have no keepers!" Holmes declared.

"That's a good one, sir!" she laughed. "So you're here to find Charlie Neff and the other two blokes, eh?"

"I must congratulate you on your ability to decipher," Holmes chortled. "Now go tell Eddie McKeeta all about us and let him know we'll be 'round for some palaver in the daylight when he's not so busy."

Millie scooted away to another table before she sashayed to the bar to refill the patrons' mugs, briefly bending the ear of her lover amidst the noise of the crowd.

"I'd wager a crown that word of our presence in this little town will spread fast, far, and wide," Holmes noted to Winchell, who was thoroughly amused by the conversation with Millie and its obvious result. "In certain matters, Mr Winchell," the consulting detective apprised, "it is wise to shake all the trees in the grove, for there is no predicting how many sweet nuts might fall to the ground."

Curiosity got the better of McKeeta. He abandoned the bar to pull up a spare chair and plop down at our table, sliding the chair backwards, straddling it, and crossing his freckled arms over the crest of the backrest. His sleeves were rolled up to his elbows and he used his right forearm to wipe the perspiration from his forehead.

"I don't want you fellas knocking at my door in the daylight, because that's when I'm in bed—I don't get outa here until four or five o'clock in the morning sometimes," he said with a grunt to open the repartee. "I'm a dainty one, and the disruption would make me even more fragile."

"Oh, Eddie, we won't have that," Holmes consoled. "Maybe your psyche can't handle some tough questions, then."

"Try me, but if I faint on ya, just lay me across the bar and have yourselves another pint," Eddie quipped.

"Prepare yourself, Eddie, here is the first: How many seafaring men from Syria have stayed in your inn over the past week?"

"How many from Syria? What gives you the idea I ask where they're from?" Eddie pressed seriously.

"Come, now, Eddie, that would be the natural question an inn-keeper would ask," Holmes shot back.

"Well, I guess I did. There were four of them—they stayed a week and checked out Tuesday. How in tarnation did you know?"

"I operate a vast intelligence network and know pretty much everything," Holmes boasted to exaggerate his prowess. "Did you hear any of their names?"

"Shipwreck! Man the lifeboats!" hollered a shadowy figure in the doorway. "A ship has run aground on Wolf Rock! I can see the distress signal from here!"

Oscar Winchell sprang from his chair and began to point at the customers. "You, you, and you, hurry to the beach!" He turned to me and Holmes. "This is what I dreaded, gentlemen. Dr Watson, we might need your help with the injured. Come with me. Mr Holmes—"

"This is what I anticipated to bring my investigation to a conclusion—soon after dawn, I swear by Poseidon," Holmes interrupted. "I am off to free the lighthouse keepers from captivity." With that, he darted toward the door and into the moonless blackness outside.

Winchell paid a young man named Alfred two shillings to take the horses back to the barn, then handed me a torch from inside the wagon bed and motioned for me to follow along a path, steep in places, for the kilometer jog to the beach. There, several skiffs were tethered and men were frantically climbing into them, raising the sails, and shoving off to reach Wolf Rock. Winchell and I joined one group as the choppy waters lapped against the small vessel, creating a motion that caused my stomach to churn. My worry over the potential to capsise increased as we gained distance to the wreckage, but we came to Wolf Rock unscathed.

The wooden front hull of the steamship *Pennsylvanian* was shredded against the volcanic fissures of the lava formation, and the freighter was taking on water, albeit slowly. We boarded the craft via a rope ladder, finding the crew stunned, scraped and bruised but otherwise not severely harmed, except for one older sailor with a broken left wrist. The captain was badly cut on the cranium because his head had crashed through the glass of the pilot house with the sudden and violent impact. I administered first aid with what medical supplies were in the emergency chest and diagnosed the captain with a concussion, ordering him to his cabin.

The pandemonium that had erupted with the collision finally subsided once all the skiffs were alongside the *Pennsylvanian* and the confused seamen were being treated for their injuries.

Captain Marshal McClure, unshaven and with a crude personality, was a stubborn sort, emerging from his quarters after about twenty minutes of confinement. "I want to oversee your methods," he protested. "My brain is throbbing, but the pain is even worse when I try to rest. Besides, I need to be assured the welfare of my crew is a priority."

"Suit yourself," I snapped, "but be forewarned, your condition is critical and activity could render you unconscious."

McClure wailed: "I knew this damn obstacle was out there, but I reckoned it was farther to the port side. What will become of my cargo, my position with the company now? I was disciplined last year for drinking too much rum, and tonight I was as sober as a preacher."

"Your miscalculation could have cost some personnel their lives, so consider yourself as having had good fortune," I groused. "Stop interfering with my duties as an attending physician and return to your cabin for the sake of your own health."

McClure stormed away, griping, and I continued examining the line of patients that stretched halfway across the afterdeck. Just then, the ship teetered to the starboard side and we all lost our balance, some falling and some staggering. The ship, now lower in the water, righted itself and I hastened my efforts, acutely aware of the possibility of it sinking with all hands on board.

It was not until the wee hours that I completed my tasks, exhausted from the stress and lack of sleep. Oscar Winchell, who had been occupied organising our rescue mission, approached me as I finished patching up the last of the crew members. He offered to let me catch a few winks on a cot in the lantern room atop the tower of the empty lighthouse. "I would appreciate it, for I am all in," I responded, following him to the skiff and then to the outcropping of Wolf Rock, then up the long, twisting iron staircase that led to the lantern room. My legs felt rubbery as we reached the pinnacle and I fell into the canvass bedding with a sigh of relief. I was in dreamland within minutes, only to be awakened as the sun touched the horizon by the muzzle of a rifle poking at my ribcage.

"Get up," the gunman snarled, his index finger on the trigger and the hammer cocked.

"Who *are* you and what is this all about?" I demanded, groggy and bewildered.

"Never mind with your stupid questions," he snarled again in an accent that sounded Middle Eastern. "Do as I say or I kill you in a second."

I obeyed and rose to my feet, mindful that my old service revolver was tucked into my belt beneath my jacket. I was determined to use my equaliser if the opportunity presented itself.

"Out," the assailant ordered, then stepped behind me when I moved toward the steps. Once on the craggy Wolf Rock, in the light of daybreak, I gawked, to my horror, at a lifeless Oscar Winchell, face up and eyes open, with a gaping exit wound in his chest and a torn shirt soaked with blood. His trusty Betsy lay askew beside him while two more attackers were dead nearby, one prostrate over his rifle and the other on his right side, gripping a pistol. I was amazed that I hadn't awakened at the sound of the gunfire. I had no idea how many more of the armed men were in the area, but I saw the craft on which they had arrived—a steam tug schooner abreast of the *Pennsylvanian* on the leeward edge of her bow. The combatants had erected a plank bridge to the crippled ship. They were directing at gunpoint the sailors and their rescuers in the transfer of goods to the schooner. There were at least ten gunmen altogether, plus another on the rock besides the one who had disrupted my sleep and kept me under close guard.

I bent over the corpse of Winchell to check for a sign of life that I knew deep down wasn't there, and then felt futilely for a pulse in the bodies of the two gunmen. "You doctor?" my captor enquired.

"Yes, I am a doctor, but I can do nothing for these three," I intoned.

"They are with many virgins in Allah's kingdom," he said proudly, pointing at his two fallen comrades. "My enemy," he sneered with pearly white teeth, motioning toward Winchell, "burns in Gehenna. I kill him, send him to hell. You enemy too?"

"I am not anyone's enemy," I insisted. "I live in peace with everyone."

"You be like woman, then," he squawked. "Woman fight with no one. Only make love. Give me your money. And your clock on chain. Gold. I trade it for more money."

"If it's money you want, here, take my billfold, but the gold watch belonged to my grandfather and I'll keep it," I argued.

He reached out and ripped the keepsake from my vest. "I take everything or you die!" the reprobate yelled.

Uncontrolled anger welled up inside me, and I lunged for the barrel of the rifle, grasping it with my left hand and forcing it off target. The firearm discharged, the bullet passing centimeters to my right. As it did, I grabbed for my revolver, withdrew it fast, and plunged it against his chest, shooting rapidly three times. My slugs struck him point blank in the heart, and he folded into a heap at my feet. The other adversary blasted a shot at me from his hip, missing as I dashed toward the lighthouse. The seamen and rescuers he was holding at bay rushed him in unison, disarmed him, and beat him onto the rugged surface of the rock. They kicked, punched, and pounded the back of his head against the hard lava while he screamed for mercy. One of the seamen, who took possession of the rifle, put a bullet through the belligerent's brain just as the cluster of six liberated hostages ran in my direction.

Some of the bandits aboard the schooner fired at us, but their aims were off due to the shifting of their boat and our speed in making our way through the lighthouse entrance for cover. Once safely inside, we placed the bar across the door and bolted it shut. Trapped but secure, we counted the cartridges for the two lever-action rifles. I knew I had three rounds of ammunition left in my handgun, and the weapon I confiscated from the robber held four more. The other rifle, an identical .45-calibre, was loaded with six in the magazine—enough to defend ourselves if we were attacked through the narrow doorway, which was the only access, because we were surrounded by the curved granite walls. I gave the Winchester to one of the rescuers, who said he was a marksman, and the three of us bearing arms stationed ourselves as sentries a few paces from the heavy oak door, our backs to the staircase. The rest of the men climbed their way to the lantern room, keeping low and away from the window that encircled the lamp.

One of the men peeked out and shouted down the stairwell that nothing resembled any movement near the schooner to indicate an assault on our position was imminent. He reported that the transfer of cargo was on-going.

"There's a man toting a crate who looks like Charlie Neff, our lighthouse keeper," the fellow added. "I guess he's alive alright."

Unexpectedly and without warning, the deafening resonance of the *Pennsylvanian* moaning and groaning penetrated our enclosure. I unbolted the door and removed the bar, poking my head out a slit of an opening to witness the huge vessel roll onto its port side. At the same time, the stern dropped into the abyss. Adversary and captive alike were catapulted overboard, some into the ocean and some against the rock outcropping. Cries for help came next from the severely injured until the horrific noise from the submerging ship drowned out their pleas. The schooner tilted back and forth, causing those aboard to fall onto the deck, several hanging onto the rail to avoid being hurled into the churning sea. Then there occurred a chilling quiet that seemed unnatural, save for the sound of the whistling wind and the bursting of bubbles where the *Pennsylvanian* had been.

My thoughts raced from Captain McClure to the multitude of merchant marines who perished, then to the bloodied souls who lived through the ordeal and needed my attention on the perimeter of Wolf Rock. Men were swimming to its edge, breathlessly, and stepping over others writhing in pain. I had foregone all concern for my own safety and ventured outside to assist those sorry individuals who were badly hurt.

A shot rang out from the schooner and the projectile struck close behind me, ricocheting away, which prompted me to retreat to the lighthouse. "These murderous outlaws are bent on revenge," I remarked excitedly to the two sentries who had stayed inside. Seven survivors who had swum to Wolf Rock joined us, dodging more bullets en route to our structure.

I scurried up to the lantern room so I could observe the combatants and I noticed two of them hoisting what appeared to be a battering ram into a dinghy, then two more with rifles jumped in.

They were coming to get us.

I descended the stairs and on the way down I devised a plan of defence, which I explained to the sentries in hurried sentences.

"When they approach the door to break it down, fling it open and blast the two riflemen to smithereens," I commanded. "I'll go back up top to see them coming, and when they reach the spot where they become most vulnerable, I'll bellow the word 'now!' at the top of my lungs."

Minutes seemed like hours, but soon the pair with the battering ram marched toward the door. The two with rifles kept pace right behind them. They halted in the shade of the tower, and as the first pair swung the battering ram backwards for momentum, I cupped my hands around my mouth and shouted the order to commence fire as loudly as I could. As the door creaked, the reports from our guns echoed through the tower when the weapons exploded in a volley. Three of the attackers collapsed where they stood. The fourth man turned to race away, but as he did, he careened face down onto the rock's sharp surface, motionless. I cheered, bounded down the steps, and darted out to gather up the two firearms. Another shot from the schooner ricocheted off the granite slab adjacent to the doorway, and I tore back inside before I was harmed.

Our arsenal was thus replenished with the two additional rifles, both loaded to the maximum. I called for two more volunteers for sentry duty from among the half-dozen men in the lantern room. Not surprisingly, each man wanted the job, but the first two down the stairs were awarded the honor. "I'm a good shooter at a distance and I can pick them off from here," said a sailor named Arnold as I handed him a Winchester.

"We can't afford wasted ammunition if you miss," I cautioned.

"I'll not miss, just you watch and see," he pledged.

Arnold leaned his left shoulder against the door jam, raised the rifle to his right shoulder, cocked his head to view the sights, steadied his left hand against the building, aimed, gently squeezed the trigger with the tip of his index finger, and held his breath until the gun responded. It boomed and recoiled slightly against his cheek.

"One down and five to go!" he snorted. "The scoundrel dropped into the water nose first, gone to lock arms with Davey Jones."

"Ship ahoy!" came a voice from the lantern room. "It's on the horizon and pointed in our direction!"

I ascended the steps to see for myself, thinking that perhaps we could signal an SOS in Morse code with a shiny object from atop the tower. Then it dawned on me: We could use the flame of the lamp, since the sky had become overcast and darkened the atmosphere sufficiently so that the light would be visible from afar. With assistance from one of the local men in the room, we ignited the flame and I draped my jacket over the lens. I removed it quickly three times to represent dots, then held it longer three times to represent dashes, then quickly three times again. I repeated the message twice after a pause of about thirty seconds in between.

As the vessel drew closer, I could see smoke billowing from its stack and hear the faint blowing of the foghorn. As it drew closer yet, I could see the flag of the Royal Navy—flapping in the breeze above an enormous battleship, which I estimated to be at least four hundred meters in length, traveling at great speed, possibly sixteen knots. There were four guns in twin turrets, one forward and one aft, on pear-shaped barbettes, plus twelve guns in casements in a pair of gun decks amidships, as well as sixteen smaller guns lining the rail. All the weapons were manned by enlisted men in uniform, who trained the intimidating battery of weapons on those aboard the steam tug schooner. The belligerents laid down their rifles and raised their hands high.

My eyes glimpsed two figures on the bridge of the battleship HMS *Majestic*, and there, standing next to the captain at the helm, was Sherlock Holmes, puffing his shag tobacco in his bent-billiard, Algerian briar-root pipe, calm as a cucumber, with his cloth deerstalker cap pushed back on his forehead.

All the occupants of the lantern room scrambled down to the entrance of the lighthouse and out into the open, free as birds on the wing. They hooted and hollered and applauded as Holmes and the captain were lowered in a rowboat that would bring them to the edge of Wolf Rock. I went over to greet them as they marveled at the carnage.

"Well, Watson, I see you have been as busy as a mother hen in a thunderstorm, wreaking havoc and doing considerable damage to a notorious gang of pirates," Holmes proclaimed, lifting his cap and scratching his scalp with his little finger.

"I believed I would never see you again," I answered clumsily.

"It is a sad thing that we lost a good man in Oscar Winchell, but I am grateful you are intact," he said to soothe my nerves.

"How in the blazes did you know the lighthouse keepers were aboard a pirate craft?" I wondered.

"I deduced it from the start," he revealed. "I read months ago in the *Times* a first-person account of a lighthouse keeper in Greece who escaped from the clutches of Mohammed Abdul and his band of thieves. They forced him into slavery aboard their steam tug schooner until he jumped ship in the Mediterranean and swam to shore in Italy, where the vicious wrongdoers were bartering for supplies with their stolen goods. It was elementary to make the connection to the affairs in Cornwall."

"What became of you after you bolted out of the Hideaway Tavern?" I wanted to know.

"Luckily, there was a midnight express to Penzance. It was there that the HMS *Majestic* was docked, I had learned before we left London," Holmes disclosed further. "I sent a message to my brother Mycroft in the Home Office, instructing him to contact the Royal Navy and advise the captain's superiors that I would probably need his help in rounding up a band of pirates. Everything fell into place afterward."

Holmes and I departed on a skiff to collect our belongings on land, pay our respects to the widow of Oscar Winchell, and return to Wolf Rock to board the HMS *Majestic* before it set sail for London with its cargo of prisoners in its brig.

Once situated in berths on the battleship, I stretched my arms out wide, yawned, and dozed momentarily, then drifted off into a restful slumber after a satisfying meal in the officers' mess.

Jack Grochot is a retired investigative newspaper journalist and a former federal law enforcement agent specializing in mail fraud cases. He lives on a small farm in southwestern Pennsylvania, where he writes and cares for five boarded horses. Besides newspaper stories, Grochot has co-written and edited a nonfiction book, *Pittsburgh Characters*, published by The Iconoclast Press of Greensburg, Pennsylvania. The author is an active member of Mystery Writers of America.

THREE SUDDEN MURDERS

by George Zebrowski

"When you come to a fork in the road, take it."
—Yogi Berra

1. ILL WITH ENEMIES

No one asked me for money and just assumed I'd show up for the ride this time of year. They always gassed up the car and did the driving.

You have to know that I was owed what I did, that I still own the justice of it, or you won't understand what happened. I don't know what that's asking of you, because I didn't understand it then or now and maybe never will.

We got into the Chevy in Hudson, New York. The shoe salesman from the town's most expensive store, who had the face of a movie actor whose name I don't remember, drove his own car. The second, a tall thin guy with a face like Buster Keaton, worked in my college cafeteria. I knew him slightly. The third guy acted like John Garfield but had never heard of him. He tried to be my friend, and lived in the basement of my off-campus apartment building. We had all been at the same college, and still got together when the salesman needed to get into the city, to see his insecure girlfriend three or four times a year, but mostly when any of us needed a ride we couldn't afford.

We set off for New York City—actually for the Westchester train station, where we would all go our separate ways, two of us with the car to a local address and two by the train into the city.

"So," said the salesman after a half hour of silence, as we faced the threat of an early 1970s Christmas, "—who got any this week?"

"I signed a book contract," I said.

You don't need the name of the publisher, or even to know if it was true or not, which it was; it won't change anything that happened, and this story works just as well with a lie or with the truth.

"What are you talking about?" Garfield asked with a sneer.

"My novel," I said, trying to remember when I had lied to him about my hopes in the past; to him and others.

"Liar," he said.

I said angrily, "Drive back and I'll get out the contract. We're not that far yet."

"But you just don't happen to have it with you—and if you do, it's a gagged up phony to show your parents."

I turned around in the passenger seat and glared at him. Stone-faced Keaton next to him said nothing. The salesman leaned closer to the wheel as I turned forward again.

It was shabby living through college with these guys back in the '70s, half out of life with vague ambitions. I looked down on them. Maybe not so much down but away, and they felt it, but we forgave a lot in those days, because we were all in the same sinking boat.

"So what's your phony story," Garfield said, brightening because he was sure that I would only talk myself deeper into the lie.

And suddenly his words made it seem that maybe I was lying. The worst accusations about me were true, and everything true was falling away from the car as it raced deeper into the gloom of evening in the hills. You get that way, and it takes a lot to shake it off, because you tend to believe the worst, as if you want to be punished for something you did way back when, and that part of you which knows you're innocent is tied up and gagged in some slippery, snail-infested dungeon at the back of your skull.

"So?" he asked behind me, without even a hint of doubt.

"It's true," I said with a needy calm.

"You wanted too much to be famous," he said.

"You saw the stories in magazines," I said.

He laughed. "Just some guy with your name."

"You can't be serious," I said.

"You're a phony," he said.

His words were a wall of genuine disbelief, bringing back all my own doubts about what I had worked so hard to get.

No one spoke up for me in the long silence. When loyalty is deserved, I told myself, you expect a friend to defend you; when undeserved, loyalty seeks justice, however painful; where loyalty is love, it acts blindly, even heroically. None of that was in the car with me. Stone-Face should have spoken up for me, but he did not.

I was losing myself again, becoming the failed version of myself that I had always feared. He had me where my worst self wanted me to be, accepting the truth as a lie.

I dozed during the rest of the trip, but my fears ran on without me, ignoring the accusation of a person who was only lashing out at his own problems and hitting an unfaithful version of myself by accident. That was all it was, and my rage was misplaced. Garfield had shot off his mouth. That was all there was to it. Let it go.

But I felt alone with him, and the car was driving itself to oblivion. The driver and Stone-Face were mannequins, so it didn't matter that the driver might well believe the liar; after all, neither he nor Stone-Face had seen any paperwork from me. I had lied to a girl five years earlier; I was being punished for that.

Then it occurred to me that I'd had to lie, if only to myself; self-fulfilling prophecies obligate you to make good before the shame catches up with you...

When the car left us off at the station, my accuser was silent, as if nothing had happened. He had been rehearsing a play. It had all been a dream. I was still asleep in the car, and the future was still waiting mercilessly for all of us.

The car drove off. It was the last I ever saw of Stone-Face and the salesman, and I wondered if they would ever know or care that I had been lied about. Would Stone-Face ever investigate? What would he think if he saw my work in a bookstore?

As we walked into the nearly deserted train station, I felt encouraged by its emptiness.

I felt him near me, and wondered how he could be silent. Was he secretly celebrating his exposure of my lies? Was the lie so settled within him? I had somehow slipped into a world where I did not belong, where I was not myself, and would never be myself again, because the lie was true.

We climbed the long stairs, each with his own suitcase, up to the outdoor station platform. Did he regret what he had said in the car? What evidence had he imagined against me, or had it been a wild guess? Stone-Face and the driver knew nothing except my bragging. Helpless, I had been unable to prove anything in the car.

I looked over at him on the long stairs to the sky. He looked away, unsure, but it was too late to take back what he had said. He had to know that he was a liar, but was hoping against it. He had to believe his own lie, certain that he had uncovered something by sheer good luck. There would be no convincing him. Even a published book would be dismissed as by someone with my name. There were people with my name. My vanity had found them out. They increased with the years. I wondered if the namesakes thought about each other, or cared. A publisher had once thrown a party for three or four such namesakes. John D. MacDonald had been irritated by Ross Macdonald's byline, despite the small d.

We came out on the concrete platform, clean in the gloom just after sunset. It calmed me with its solidity and lack of stains. How often did they clean it to keep that gray?

We stood there alone, waiting for the train into New York City. He was grinning at me as if nothing had happened. I looked away and thought of Stone-Face and the driver. Both my friends, by degrees; but they had not stood up for me. They had been silent in the car, and would stay so forever, believing that the lie had been an unmasking of some kind, a king's-invisible-new-clothes event. A lie well told might never be refuted, an urgent legend—an urban legend, of course—like later sightings of dead peoples' twins or ghosts. People believe what they want to believe about you, Sinatra had once said. I am not a crook, Nixon had said.

Garfield stepped toward the edge of the platform and looked west. The gloomy evening air was thick with smog. A whistle blew, and we saw the train's light shining through like a small approaching sun. It brightened into a blinding intensity.

When it passed, and my eyes adjusted, I was alone on the platform.

I had killed him long before my hands reached out and my fear said push.

I have no memory of it. I got on the train and rode into the city, expecting for some weeks after to be questioned, but no one came; the fall had happened so close to the moment that the motorman, if he had been looking, did not have time to see.

I might have had to say that I tried to catch my friend as he stumbled, but no one asked. He was a friend, I would have told them, but not close enough to repeat it, if anyone had asked. I did not push him, I would have said, but no one cared enough to let me deny it.

I cared more when I heard about the mangled body that was found, and no one knew what had happened. Maybe a suicide.

He might have been a great sports announcer, I imagined as I waited, even though he hated Damon Runyon stories. How many people don't get to be what they wanted to be, or even might have been? Best known for becoming a body on a track, but he might have been better known as a friend of the author who knew him waybackwhen in their wannabe days. What had I stopped with his heart? If he had come to nothing, I might have been there to gloat, up in some future; but if he had become an accomplished sort, I would have been there to congratulate, or ignore him…

I had pushed off from everything I had known, and would now live as what I had become…wearing the everyday that would never be the same again. Everything was a fraud, I thought, as I saw his broken body and the unremembered impulse that had brought him his sudden stillness and had taken me along with him as if some-one had pulled a puppet string hooked deep inside me, releasing all that I had needed to put my hand on his back and push, all too quickly for me to vomit up my heart.

Would I be able to live with it?

A clean hate of cold forgiveness had taken me through it.

Would I live with it?

Two weeks later the publisher cancelled my book contract. My agent told me that they didn't want the first half of the advance back, but he told me I should pay it back anyway. They fired my editor, who died the following week, and my agent let me go be-fore I could fire him. Garfield grinned at me from the grave.

I found another agent, and another publisher, and lived past the delay…

But in the endless police silence I sat in my room, waiting to see something crawl across the carpet, crablike, roachlike, at least the size of a baseball.

Briefly, the truth had become a lie, then struggled and righted itself. Revenge did not sicken me. The death of my enemy left me with only one regret—that now I couldn't kill him again.

I thought of Stone-Face, who had not defended me in the car. Had he imagined that I had been exposed? He had hoped that it was true.

He would have to pay for that.

✗   ✗   ✗   ✗

Once in a while people need to kill each other.
—Anonymous

2. KAYAK

Ethan sat on the porch and watched his wife swimming in the lake. Isabel could keep it up forever, swim, tread, and float all day, as if she had been born in the water and was determined to live there; when she left him, that's where she would be. There was nothing he could do about it in the summers except wait for her to come out, be ready to throw her a life preserver or maybe even to dive in after her if she needed any help. Drylanders were obligated to the waterfolk…

The water shimmered in the late afternoon sun because the diamonds on its surface refused to sink.

A strenuous kayaker came up behind her, oars flying as if he expected to take off and fly, disrupting the glittering carpet of unsinkable gems, and hit her in the head. She sank. The oarsman windmilled away as if nothing had happened.

Ethan was off the porch after what seemed an eternity of effort, down the path to the dock and into the water, splashing more than swimming, looking for her beneath a surface that had become a wall that had fallen over her.

She bobbed up, head down. He grabbed her hair and lifted her head. She coughed, but there was blood in her red hair. He sank for a moment, then came up and pulled her to shore, past the dock, and hauled her out by the shoulders.

She lay breathing on the sandy mud. But what was breathing? What was left inside the bloody head?

He looked away and spotted the blue kayak in the distance. A blond man was flipping the oar, glancing back anxiously as he pulled away.

Ethan looked around for the binoculars that Isabel used for checking out the ducks on the far shore, then saw that her chest had stopped moving.

He was at her side, starting to work on her, when he saw the blood soaking into the sand. She had not drowned; she had been bludgeoned to death.

But he tried for the next quarter hour, breathing into her and fooling himself that he saw her chest move, then sat back on his heels in shock, unable to think, watching her stillness, expecting it to end…

At last he got to his feet, and stood shaking, then staggered up to the house, called the ambulance, and went back.

Kneeling, he kissed her cold lips and held her head in his lap as he waited for the helpless help to arrive.

He gave his statement to the lone policeman who showed up a century after the ambulance had left.

The graying cop looked at him in the fading daylight of the kitchen, then stepped back and asked, "You sure she was hit by a kayak oar and didn't just drown?"

"What?" Ethan said and stepped toward him. "Why, just go and look at the body!"

"Oh, yeah, sorry I missed the wagon. Have to ask. People tell me all sorts of things, you know."

"Go look!"

"Okay, okay, I'm sorry."

Ethan tried to calm himself, outraged by the effort.

"They told you she was dead?" the cop asked, moving his jaw as if he were chewing gum.

"Well no…but."

"I'll double check."

"She wasn't breathing!"

"Okay, but how close did you look? Okay, okay. I'll get on it."

"Hurrying won't help," Ethan said, and the cop grimaced at him, then let the door slam as he left.

Ethan sat down and wondered how he could ever be calm again as he began to hear a rushing in his ears.

After what seemed like hours he put on his jeans, shirt, and boots, found his phone and hung the binoculars around his neck, and went out to his pickup.

He drove south slowly along the shore, looking for blue and blond among the vacationers, wishing that he had caught the man's face in the binoculars and imprisoned it in the lenses for all time.

He searched the shores as if somehow he might find her instead of her killer, remembering how it had been whenever they were apart: a kind of relief, for a day or two; but on the third or fourth day it would begin to suck, and now it would suck forever—whether he found her killer or not.

Isabel was away. His feelings insisted that she would be back; it could not mean anything else, because that was the way it had always been between them. She had never been away like this, or in any other way...so it would never be different.

Toward evening, when he had nearly driven the entire irregular lakeshore, he slowed down.

Blue and blond.

A blue kayak was beached on the sand. A blond man stood nearby with a beer in his hand.

Ethan stopped and cut his engine.

The man heard him and turned around.

Ethan sat watching him. The blond man stared back.

Finally, the man started to walk toward his bungalow.

Ethan got out of the truck and slammed the door, and the man began to run, dropping his beer.

Ethan called out, "Gotta talk to you!"

The man tripped halfway to the door and Ethan caught up with him. As Ethan looked down at him, the man's legs twisted and tried to get him up. He was breathing hard, avoiding Ethan's gaze, looking around at the red sand as if trying to find his dropped beer. Ethan remembered when the community had met to decide on the purchase of the sand for the beaches, but he did not recall this man showing up for the vote.

Ethan took a deep breath and asked, "Why?"

The man stayed down, rose up on one elbow, then went down on his back, as if trying to look helpless. He was young, Ethan saw, maybe not even twenty.

"Well?" Ethan asked, giving him a small kick in the shin.

The man started to weep. "I don't know, man! It just came over me."

Ethan squatted and stared at the blubbering face.

"You don't know?" he asked. "How can you not know!"

"Yeah, I don't know. You tell me!"

"How would I know?" Ethan asked, feeling the acid inside him along with the terror in the young man's face.

"Somebody's gotta know," said the young man.

Ethan looked at the man and knew that the boy was not a killer—who had killed.

Ethan took his cell phone from his belt, dialed the hospital and asked about his wife. Yes, Isabel was dead, double checked by the cop's doubts.

The young man on the sand had closed his eyes, but opened them when Ethan finished his call.

"She's dead," Ethan said.

"Go ahead, kill me," said the young man. "No one will ever convict you."

"You studying law?"

"No—plumbing. My father wants me to go in with him."

"And?"

"I hate him, and all pipes."

Ethan looked at him, unable to speak because there was nothing waiting to be said; both their lives had run out of words to say to each other.

"I can't…" said the young man, "ever live with…this."

Ethan knew that only forgetfulness would be of use, but only one kind was truly available to the young man—and none for himself. There was nothing left, and nothing after…

Ethan was glad that he was wearing boots as he stepped up to the man's head and kicked.

✗　✗　✗　✗

3. UNSAFE

Sprawled on the sofa, one intruder held a gun on the old couple in their comfy chairs while his partner searched the house.

The searcher came back after a noisy half hour, looking disappointed.

"Nothing," he said to his gun-pointing partner. "All they have is books, in every room, DVDs, CDs, crap like that."

"What's with you?" asked the lounger. "Don't you people have anything?"

The couple was silent.

"Well?"

"We sold all our good stuff a long time ago," said the handsome old woman, "so this is all we have. Take the television and stereo."

"This stuff's all…so old. Where's your flat screen, or your Bose sound system?"

"We never earned much," said the woman.

"What did you do?"

"We write for a living," she said.

"Really? Writers, huh? Damn little money in that."

"For most," said the husband.

"One thing," said the tired searcher as he sat down in a worn upholstered chair. "There's a rusty old safe under the basement stairs. Disgusting with dust."

"Oh?" said the gunman, sitting forward. "What's in it?"

"Nothing," said the woman.

He pointed the gun at the old man. "Whaddya say I shoot him in the shoulder?"

"You can say it," she said, "but the safe will still be empty."

"How's about we see for ourselves?"

The searcher had closed his eyes and was leaning back in his chair. "There's nothing here, Henry," he said. "Let's get going."

"Why don't you give them my address," Henry said.

"Hey," shouted the husband, "James Cagney said that in *White Heat*!"

"No, dear," said the woman, "that was Cagney in *Shake Hands With The Devil*, just before he shot the captive Black and Tan policeman."

"It's a common enough name, Henry," the searcher said as he opened his eyes. "What's a black and tan?"

"So give them your name, too," Henry said. "The cops will show them pictures, you know."

"My name's Bob," the searcher said, "so I guess we'll have to kill them."

"Okay," Henry said, "you're nice old folks, and goddamned writers, too, so just give me the combination."

"Give *us*, the combination," Bob said. "There are two of us here."

"A comedy act," said the writer to his wife.

"There is no combination," said the woman. "The safe was from long before our twenty years here."

"I told you," said her husband, "to have it opened professionally and leave it open, so this wouldn't have a chance of happening."

"No tricks," said the gunman as he shifted the weapon to his left hand. "What's the combo!"

"Don't have it," said the woman.

"How's we don't believe you," said Bob.

"Did you ever open it?" asked Henry.

"Nope," said her husband. "By the way, I'm Crawford, and this is my wife Prunella."

"I get the Prunella," said Henry, "but is Crawfish your first or last name?"

"First," Crawford said.

Bob guffawed and sat back. "I gotta hear their last name."

The couple were silent.

"Well?" asked Henry.

"Tell them," Prunella said, "so they can die laughing."

"The combination, wise-ass," Henry said, extending his gun toward her.

"Now, young man," Prunella said in a motherly way, "you know that you are not going to shoot me."

"Oh, yeah? You really *know* that?"

"He doesn't know himself," Bob added.

"If I die, you won't get the combination."

"Oh, so there is one," Henry said.

"Maybe, and my husband doesn't know it."

"His shoulder, lady, will never be the same."

Prunella said, "But, really, sonny, there is no combination."

"So you say."

"He'll shoot," Bob said and Henry grinned at her.

"Whatever made you boys so nasty?" Prunella asked. "I don't believe you can do it. You don't have it in you."

"Hey," cried the husband, "that was Zero Mostel, the crooked shyster in *The Hot Rock!*"

"Quite right this time, dear," she said, "but he wasn't all that crooked."

"Crooked enough," her husband said, "to know better about everything in the movie."

"Who do you think you people are?" Henry cried. "You talk as if you owned the friggin' world. Enough with the product placement."

"Crawford Kane and Prunella Angleton," her husband said, "if you read books. Writers are like that."

"You have separate names?" Bob asked. "Damn."

"Sure," Crawford said, "we treasure our bylines."

"Bylines?" Henry asked.

"You know, the name that goes in front of whatever you write," Crawford said.

"Oh, yeah, sure. But Prunella? Who'd want to read a Prunella?"

"You can do other things with a Prunella," Bob said, eyeing her knees.

"But people do remember the name," she said.

"The combination, lady," Bob said, "or…Crawford will need a new shoulder—if he lives to get one."

"Let's take this down to the basement," Henry said, standing up. "It'll inspire them."

The two young men went down to the basement, and stood watching as the old couple crept down the old wooden stairs and sat down in the small laundry room sofa.

The big old metal box waited smug and safe under the stairs.

The two intruders stood looking at the big door.

"Okay, lady," said the gunman, "open it."

She went over to the safe and stood with her back to the two men. Slowly, she grasped the handle, and opened the door.

"Hey!" Bob shouted.

"Sure," she said as she looked inside, "but we never tried it, so how could we know it was open?"

"Clean forgot," said her husband.

Henry tucked his gun into his belt.

Prunella waited a moment, then turned around with a German Lugar in her right hand.

"Look what I found inside, dear," she said to her husband, who blinked and sat back, creaking the cheap old sofa's springs as he adjusted his baggy pants.

Henry drew his gun and she fired. He dropped the gun and collapsed with a small hole in his chest. Bob screamed and backed away, bumping into the washing machine.

She waited until he was quiet. They all looked down at the man on the green floor.

"He's not breathing," Crawford said.

"Now, Bob, listen carefully," Prunella said.

"What?" Bob asked, horrified by her calm.

"You're going to run away," she said.

"You'll shoot me!" he cried, looking around for his gun. Crawford put out his foot and kicked the gun away into the corner by the washing machine.

"I won't have to," Prunella said.

"You will!" he cried.

"No, I won't," she said. "Your friend is dead, and it's his own fault. You'll get to live, and you'll never say a word about what happened here. You won't want to confess how you broke in to rob us at gunpoint."

Her husband said, "It's too complicated to let him go."

Prunella thought about it and said, "I was hoping he would be… too honest to ever speak of it—but you're probably right."

The corpse was bleeding red onto the green floor.

"I'll dig a hole in the vegetable cellar," her husband said, "pave it over and paint it green."

"Perfect," Prunella said. "I like green."

"Let me go!" Bob cried.

Prunella stepped aside and motioned to the open safe with the Lugar. "Get in," she said.

"No!" Bob cried. "There won't be air!"

Her husband said, "You'd better shoot him. I can get two in the grave."

"No, no!" Bob cried, moving toward the safe. He bent down to get in and stopped. "It's too small."

"In on your ass and bring your knees up inside," Prunella said. Bob hesitated.

"Or get shot," she said. "Headshot is quick."

"We'll stuff the stiff in," her husband said.

Bob got in and peered out at her. "You'll let me out, won't you? After you've buried him…you could just tie me up before you call the cops."

"Maybe," she said and closed the door. It clicked, and she whirled the combination.

She went over and sat down next to her husband, and put the Lugar down on the floor. After a moment, they heard knocking from inside the safe. It became more frequent.

An hour later, they heard nothing.

"They shouldn't have threatened to shoot you," she said.

"Did you know the gun was in the safe?" he asked, looking at the body.

"No."

He picked up the Lugar and checked the clip.

"You know about this model?" she asked.

He sighed. "Yeah, it's mine."

"Yours?"

"A souvenir from the war."

"So you knew the safe was open?"

"A long time ago, when I wanted to get rid of the gun, I found the combination scratched on the side. Must have left it open last time I oiled the gun."

"Oiled the gun?" she asked.

"Yeah, I thought I might need it."

"You were right," she said.

"Yeah, I thought sometimes, when times were bad, that maybe I'd use it on myself."

She looked at him with tears in her eyes, and put her arms around him. "Oh, Crawford! And you'd leave me behind?"

"That would be up to you…later," he said.

He looked at his hands when she let him go, then wiped them on the old sofa. "Good thing I kept the gun well oiled," he said, smiling.

They sat in silence. Finally, he said, "You know, it'll make a good story."

"Which no one will believe," she said.

They looked at the body. "I'd better go get the shovel," he said.

"Have enough cement?" she asked.

"Plenty," he said. "You know, we may be long dead before anyone finds out about this."

"I'll scratch off the combination," she said.

"No need," he said, "I'll dig for two."

"Why?" she asked.

"Unsafe to leave him in the safe," he said.

About George Zebrowski

Science fiction writer Greg Bear calls George Zebrowski "one of those rare speculators who bases his dreams on science as well as inspiration." Zebrowski has published about a hundred works of short fiction, more than a hundred and forty articles and essays, and has written about science for *Omni Magazine*. His short fiction and essays have appeared in *Analog, Asimov's Science Fiction, Amazing Stories, The Magazine of Fantasy & Science Fiction, Science Fiction Age, Nature*, the *Bertrand Russell Society News, World Literature Today, Free Inquiry*, and other publications.

His best known novel is *Macrolife*. *Library Journal* chose *Macrolife* as one of the one hundred best science fiction novels. His short fiction has been nominated for the Nebula Award and the Theodore Sturgeon Memorial Award. His novel *Stranger Suns* (1991) was a *New York Times* Notable Book of the Year.

The Killing Star (1995), written with scientist/author Charles Pellegrino, was described by *The New York Times Book Review* as "a novel of such conceptual ferocity and scientific plausibility that it amounts to a reinvention of that old Wellsian staple, [alien invasion]..." *Brute Orbits* (1998) was praised by Paul Di Filippo in *Asimov's Science Fiction*, and in *Publishers Weekly*. The book won the John W. Campbell Memorial Award for Best Novel of the Year. *Cave of Stars*, a novel that is part of his Macrolife mosaic, was published in 1999.

Other books include *Skylife*, an anthology edited by Zebrowski with Gregory Benford (2000), and the collections *Swift Thoughts* (2002). *Synergy SF: New Science Fiction*, the fifth volume of his Synergy series of original anthologies, was published in 2004. *Black Pockets and Other Dark Thoughts*, with an introduction by Howard Waldrop, came out in 2006. Golden Gryphon published his horror novel *Empties* in 2009. *Sentinels In Honor of Arthur C. Clarke*, an anthology of fiction and nonfiction edited with Gregory Benford, was published in 2010 by Hadley Rille Books. His new collection, *Decimated: Ten Science Fiction Stories*, with Jack Dann, was published in 2012 by The Borgo Press/Wildside Press.

THE ADVENTURE OF THE VANISHED VILLAGE

by Michael Mallory

"**M**issy, what on earth have you done to this chop?" I asked, while attempting to cut into the leathery, snuff-coloured object that had once been a perfectly good lamb cutlet.

"Sorry, mum," she replied sullenly. "I guess I left it in the oven too long. Shall I get rid of it?"

Since none of my shoes were in need of resoling, I encouraged her to do so. I requested instead that she instead bring me a cut or two from the cold joint left over from yesterday and some cheese. With a curt bob, she disappeared into the kitchen. Whatever was I going to do with this girl? Of late, her attention to her duties had been even more scattered than usual due to her affections having been rejected by a young solicitor named Wilmer, with whom she had become smitten. After the man proved to be an unmitigated cad, she had not been able to recover from the experience, despite my attempts to help her. I was therefore encouraged when I saw her return to the dining room with a perfectly prepared plate of beef and stilton, neither of which had been bathed in mustard. Perhaps the idiomatic tide was beginning to turn. I had no sooner finished my meal and requested a cup of coffee when the doorbell rang.

"Ooh, you don't suppose it's him, do you mum?" Missy asked, excitedly.

"Dr Watson? Of course not." My husband was presently in New York, meeting with a new American publisher eager to bring forth more collections of heavily-enhanced stories chronicling John's exploits with his great and annoying friend Mr Sherlock Holmes.

"No, mum, I didn't mean the doctor, I mean *him*, Mr Wilmer."

Oh dear. "I rather hope it is your Mr Wilmer, Missy, so I can chase him down the street with the teakettle."

"Oh, no, mum…"

The doorbell rang once more, its insistent peal this time betraying the impatience of the ringer. "Dear, would you please answer the door before whoever it is breaks the bell?"

With a sigh, she shuffled off to the door and returned a moment later in the company of a man of roughly thirty years of age by my estimation. He was tall and lean, smartly dressed, and wore a felt hat of the style popularized by His Majesty, as well as neatly-trimmed side whiskers, which helped to obscure what appeared to be a small duelling scar on the left side of his face. A young professional man, I imagined, no doubt here to consult with John, but who was fated to be disappointed by his absence. "You are Amelia Watson?" he asked.

"I am. To whom am I speaking?"

"My name is Benedict McCrory. Martha Hudson sent me."

Dear Martha; the landlady of 221B Baker Street, John's former residence, still sent people around to consult with him. "How do you do, Mr McCrory?" I said. "If you have come to see Dr Watson, I am afraid he is not in. He is abroad, and will not return for a fortnight or so."

"No ma'am, I'm not here to see the doctor. I first went to Baker Street to see Mr Holmes—"

"Well, I can assure you *he* is not here, either, nor do I have any idea where he might be." I chose not to perpetuate the story that Sherlock had retired to the coast to raise ants, or whatever it was he claimed to be doing, because I knew it to be untrue. Instead my distant cousin (yes, some time back I had come to learn that Sherlock Holmes, his brother Mycroft, and I all share a family tree, albeit a somewhat knotty one) was off secretly working on cases that held a more personal attachment for him.

"Mrs Watson, you misunderstand me," the man persisted. "I am here to see you."

"Me?"

"Yes, Mrs Hudson said that in the absence of Sherlock Holmes, you were the next best thing."

Oh, good heavens! I confess that I have found myself involved in a number of adventures in the years since I became Mrs John H. Watson, the second woman to hold that title, but I really had no intention of hanging a consulting detective shingle facing Queen Anne Street. Still, the man had gone out of his way to come here;

it would be discourteous not to at least hear his story. "Jewel that Martha is, she is nevertheless given to occasional fits of exaggeration," I told him. "However, if you would care to take a seat and explain your problem, I will see if I can offer some small measure of advice." Most likely it would be *Go to the police*.

At my invitation, Mr McCrory settled into an arm chair, while Missy, *not* at my invitation, took it upon herself to plop down onto the settee where she regarded the young gentleman with wide eyes and a smile. I was on the verge of dismissing her, but deduced from her expression that I would have more success dismissing London Bridge from the Thames.

"Well, where to begin?" Mr McCrory said. "Mrs Watson, do you happen to be familiar with the small ancient village in the county of East Riding of Yorkshire called Clytendom Odd?"

"No."

"I had not heard of it either until a customer at our bank, Mr Everett, mentioned it."

"Ooh, you're a banker?" Missy cooed.

"Well, a senior clerk," Mr McCrory replied, smiling at her, which in turn caused Missy to emit a slight squeal. This was turning into a situation that warranted close watching. "Anyway, Mr Everett often spoke about the village. It seems that in the 18th century, Clytendom Odd was a place of operation for a smuggling ring given its close proximity to the seashore. Mr Everett knew this because his four-times-grand uncle, a man named Paxton, had been one of the smugglers, and this Paxton recorded details of his illicit activities in a diary, which came into Mr Everett's possession some years ago. The diary details how the Royal Navy began to suspect smugglers were working through Clytendom Odd, so they suspended activities and laid low, hoping to avoid detection. Unfortunately, it was not to be. They were captured and brought to justice, all except for Mr Everett's forebear, who managed to escape, but who lived the rest of his life in apprehension that his earlier misdeeds would be unearthed. So when the fellow realized he was nearing the end of his life, he wrote down his history so that his descendents might have a record of his activities. I suppose it was a way of asking for atonement from loved ones, and…"

Heavens! I felt as though I should be taking notes. "Forgive me, Mr McCrory," I interrupted, "I do not wish to be rude, but for all of this you have not explained why you are here."

"Oh, right. Did I mention that Mr Everett has passed on?"

"No, you did not."

"A tragedy, though he had been ill for quite some time. Too ill, in fact, to make the trip to Clytendom Odd himself. It was his greatest desire to see the place that Paxton had written about. I made the trip for him and took photos of the place with my Brownie. I'm something of an amateur photographer. Have you ever used one, Mrs Watson? They're quite light and portable, and—"

"Mr McCrory, could you please come to the point?"

"Oh, sorry. Well, soon after Mr Everett's death I received a package in the mail from his solicitor. It contained Paxton's diary accompanied by a note saying that Mr Everett wished me to have it since I had gone out of my way to bring the village to him through these photographs. I was, of course, pleased, but it was something else in the package, something stuck between the pages of the diary."

"What?" Missy asked eagerly.

"A map. You see, according to Paxton, the smugglers began to realize that the Navy was on to them, so they decided to cease activities and lie low for a while. They went so far as to take all their spoils, thousands of pounds worth of silver and gold, according to the diary, and hide it within the village of Clytendom Odd, so none of the smugglers would be caught in possession of the loot. Then they were rounded up, all except for Paxton, of course."

"So it's a treasure map?" Missy gasped.

"Quite, and with it was a personal note from Mr Everett, written on his death bed, saying, 'I give this to you, my only friend, as I do not wish my family to have it.' I believe he and his family were not on good terms, but we often see that when estates are in question."

"So," I broke in, "you have come here in hopes that I am in possession of a good shovel with which you can start digging?"

"No, madam. I sought out Sherlock Holmes, unsuccessfully as it turned out, and have now come here to you because after receiving the map, I journeyed back to Clytendom Odd."

"Did you find the treasure?" Missy asked.

"No. Neither did I find the village."

"I'm sorry?" I said.

He looked at me with earnest eyes. "It's not there, Mrs Watson. The entire village of Clytendom Odd has vanished."

"Crikey," Missy said, "no wonder they call it odd."

"Mr McCrory, how can a village simply vanish?"

"All I know is that where there used to be a village is now only an abandoned station and a terminus roundhouse. Even the road that spanned the few miles from the station to the village was nowhere to be found. In an attempt to prove to myself that my wits had not similarly disappeared, I started walking in what I was certain was the proper direction for the village. I made it all the way to the sea, but I found no village, nor any buildings, fences, foundations, or any other sign of the place ever having been inhabited. I was exhausted by the time I got back to the station, and had to wait two hours for the next train to arrive, be turned around, and take me back."

"Mr McCrory, this tale is incredible."

"I know, it sounds impossible, yet it is true," he replied. "This is why I sought out Mr Holmes. I have to know how a village can simply vanish. The conundrum has nearly driven me mad."

"When was the last time you actually saw the village?" I asked.

"A little over a year ago when I went on behalf of Mr Everett. I wouldn't have called the place a thriving village, but it was there. What can you tell me, ma'am?"

"I simply don't know what to tell you, other than suggest you contact the Yorkshire constabulary, or perhaps the railway office."

"I already have. The man at the railway office told me there had once been a Clytendom Odd, but it ceased to exist so long ago that nobody remembered it. Yet I was there last year."

"Oh, mum, doesn't this case interest you a little?" Missy asked.

"Missy, a *case* is what I keep my travel toiletries in, not the object of my attention. Mr McCrory, I am really not a consulting detective, no matter what Martha might have told you. I am sorry you have wasted your time by coming here."

With an expression of defeat, Benedict McCrory rose. "Well, I would not say coming here was a complete waste, since I was able to make the acquaintance of such two charming women." He glanced over at Missy and smiled, and I feared that she might swoon. "Your name is Missy?" he asked.

"It's short for Mistletoe," the girl replied and once again I quietly marvelled at the cruelty of her parents.

"Mistletoe, what a lovely name. I hope you won't think I am being forward, but might I call upon you sometime?"

"Yes!" the girl all but shouted.

"We shall see," I responded. "Go about your chores, now, dear, I will show Mr McCrory out myself." Leading him to the front door, I said, "I do trust that your intentions are honourable, sir."

"Of course, Mrs Watson," he said, looking cut to the quick. "I simply find her a charming young lady, I did not mean to—"

I held my hand up to silence him. "She has recently had her heart broken, and as I am responsible for her, I do not wish to see any further distress caused her."

"On my honour, madam, I intend no distress. But would it be all right if I were to call again?"

"We shall see. Good night, Mr McCrory."

As it turned out, we saw him the very next day when the young man reappeared to ask if he might escort Missy to the theatre on the following evening. Since I have long felt that Missy's indoctrination into the arts had been somewhat lacking, I agreed and almost immediately came to regret it since from the moment of my approval she became as useless in her duties as a milk cow, her head being transported to a cloud shaped like a bank clerk. Even so, when the next evening came around, I helped her prepare for her night out, all the while telling her precisely what I expected of her. "I know what time the theatres let out," I said, as she primped in front of the dressing table mirror, "so do not presume that you will be able to stay out until all hours of the morning under the excuse that the play ran long."

"Right, mum."

"What is he taking you to see?"

"*When Knights Were Bold.*"

While hardly *Hamlet*, it would have to do. "Very well," I said. "I expect you back no later than midnight."

"You're worse than me own mum, mum."

"I suppose I am," I said, smiling, "and I really do want you have a wonderful time, but please be back promptly."

Mr McCrory arrived some twenty minutes later, looking fairly resplendent if a shade uncomfortable in evening wear. A white boutonniere was pinned to his silk lapel, and he had traded his fashionable homburg for a silk opera hat. Missy was not quite up to his level of fashion, though wearing her finest dress, and with her hair arranged in proper fashion, she cut a striking figure. "Remember what I told you, dear," I said as they were about to leave.

I might as well have saved my breath.

When Missy had not arrived back home by the stroke of midnight, I was not terribly surprised since, despite my exhortations, I expected her to be slightly late. Pulling my copy of *Barnaby Rudge* down from the shelf, I settled onto the chaise and began to read, but soon, I fear, fell asleep. When I awoke, sunlight was streaming into the room.

I rose, somewhat disoriented, and called for Missy but received no reply. The girl was most likely still asleep, having gotten home late and crept in so as not to awaken me and receive a lecture. Looking at the clock, I saw it was half-past-six. Stiff and uncomfortable from having spent the night in my clothing, I made my way to Missy's room and knocked on the door. There was no answer. Going in, I found out why: there was no Missy. "Oh, good god!" I cried, and began going through each room of the house shouting for the girl. She was nowhere to be found. A terrifying thought came to me: surely the girl would not have run off with the man and eloped! I endeavoured not to panic, knowing that it was equally likely they had gone somewhere after the theatre and Mr McCrory had talked her into a stupor.

I had to release myself from this corset and dress, at least for a while, so I went to my bedroom to freshen up and change clothing and attempt to relax, even as my anger toward Benedict McCrory was growing. I had no sooner finished relacing my shoes when the doorbell rang. Dashing down, I prayed that it would be Missy and not a policeman here to report that something had befallen her. But as I swung open the front door, I did not see my maid. Instead I saw Benedict McCrory, his face flushed, his suit torn and dirty, an expression of terror on his face. "Good god, what has happened to you?" I cried. "Where is Missy?"

"Please, I need to come in," he panted.

Leading him up the stairs, I again asked what had happened.

"Do you have any whisky?" he asked.

"My husband does. Sit down here." I lowered him into the chair as I fetched a whisky from John's liquor cabinet, which Mr Mc-Crory gulped down. "Young man, where is my maid?" I demanded.

"They have her."

"*They*?"

"Two men with revolvers."

"Good lord!"

"We left the theatre and were heading for a coffee shop just to talk and they appeared out of nowhere. Big men, both armed. One demanded the map. It think they were family members of Mr Elliot. They must have been following me, waiting for their chance. I had the map on me because Missy wanted to see it. They abducted us and forced us into a carriage, saying that we had to accompany them to Clytendom Odd because that was their only way of ensuring we would not go to the police."

"Yet here you are."

"Yes. They blindfolded us and took us to a vacant building somewhere, and tied us up in chairs—"

"Good lord!"

"—and said we would be held there until the first train left for Clytendom Odd the next morning. I told them that there was no Clytendom Odd, but they only laughed. We spent most of the night there. I tried to comfort Missy as best I could, but she kept crying, 'Please, mum, come save me.'"

I sank down on the chaise and put my head in my hands. "Why did they release you?" I asked.

"They didn't. I escaped."

"And you left Missy there?" I cried.

"I managed to wriggle out of my bonds and was endeavouring to release her when I heard the men coming back. So I told her not to worry, I would bring help. I would go to the police. But she said no, that I should come and see you instead."

Dear god! "Where is this building?"

"I don't know," he said. "Once I got out through a window, I started running and didn't even think about looking at street signs. I ran and ran and ran and managed to find my way here."

"No, sir, you ran away leaving a defenceless girl in the hands of two armed blackguards!"

"If I only had a sword, Mrs Watson, I might have been able to take them, as I am quite handy with one but I did not and they had pistols. But please try to understand, had I stayed there and gone with them, I might have been killed once they found the treasure. So might Missy have been. But they wouldn't dare kill her now since I can identify them. You see?"

"What I see is that this is a matter for the police."

"And tell them that Missy has been abducted by two men who are taking her to a place that does not exist? By the time we convinced them we were not candidates for Bedlam, it would be too late to do any good."

Unfortunately the man had a point. "What do you suggest we do, then?"

"Go up there ourselves and find her."

"You are suggesting that we dash off to a place that does not exist."

"I am suggesting that we follow the men who have Missy no matter where they end up."

"Dear god," I muttered, shaking my head as I rose and went to the bookshelf. "Where does John keep his Bradshaw?"

"Bradshaw?" Mr McCrory said.

"Of course, the railway timetable...ah, there it is." I pulled the rail booklet down and saw that it was the 1902 edition—John had not bought a new one in the four years we have been married—and I hoped the passage of time did not make it obsolete. "Where in Yorkshire is this place again?" I asked, flipping through the pages.

"East Riding. The nearest large town is Kingston-upon-Hull."

"Here it is. Oh, dear. The first train has already left. Another one leaves in a little over an hour from now."

"Then we must be on it."

"Mr McCrory, I hope you will not take this personally, but I wish you had found Sherlock Holmes instead of me."

"I'm sorry, madam. But in the meantime could I trouble you for...I mean, I have been tied up most of the night and I rather have to...well..."

"The lavatory is downstairs at the end of the hall."

As the man dashed away, I sat back down and tried to think but was having a difficult time of it. Then it suddenly came to me: Mr McCrory's insight into not involving the police might be sound, but there was one person I could involve, though it would not be a call I placed lightly. Going to John's dreaded telephone, a noisome device that I normally try to avoid using, I turned the crank and waited for the operator's voice to come through the dynamite stick receiver, and then asked for a specific number, one that had been given to me in strictest confidence. After a single ring, a man's hushed voice answered, asking: "Who calls?"

"This is Mrs Amelia Watson," I said. "I need to speak with Mycroft."

"Mycroft?" he repeated, suspiciously.

"Yes, Myc…oh, I mean M, of course."

"Your name again?"

"Mrs Amelia Watson," I pronounced slowly, assuming the man would then check my name against a list. I knew full well there was a good reason for this. In the time that I have been acquainted with the brothers Holmes, even before learning that we were distant relations, it had become evident that Mycroft was a man so vital to the continuing operation of His Majesty's government that were he to die, it would have a far greater impact upon the management of the Empire than the passing of King Edward himself, god forbid. I also knew that Mycroft recently organized a special operation within the Home Office called "M Division," which was responsible for gathering clandestine intelligence; in other words, a spy unit. I knew all this because Mycroft had asked me to join M Division as an operative, heaven help me.

The man's voice came back, considerably brightened, and said, "Oh, Mrs Watson, yes, how are you?"

"Not at my best, I fear," I said. "I must talk to My…to M at once. It is quite urgent."

"I am sorry, ma'am, but M is away."

"Away? He hardly ever moves, let alone goes away." Mycroft Holmes may have possessed one of the most active minds in Britain, but there are oaks in the forest that displayed more physical movement.

"I am sorry, ma'am, but he is indeed away on business. Might I be of service to you?"

"Oh, I suppose it shan't hurt to tell you." As concisely as I could, I relayed the story of Mr McCrory's appearance at my house and why he had come, at which time the man on the line interrupted me with, "I'm sorry, did you say Clytendom Odd?"

"Yes, Clytendom Odd. I had never heard of the place before this fellow showed up."

"I see. Go on, ma'am."

In short order, I got to the crux of the problem, Missy's abduction and why I daren't call the police. "According to Mr McCrory," I emphasized, "these men threatened to harm Missy or worse if the police became involved. Oh, this is all my fault!"

"How so, ma'am?"

"I gave Missy permission to go with the man to the theatre. Had I not, she would be here and safe. But he seemed like a decent sort of fellow, albeit one who apparently carries his bravery only in a scabbard."

"I don't follow."

"Oh, he professes to be adept with a sword and even has a scar to prove it, but…oh, never mind. What's done cannot be undone."

"Given what you have told me, I will send word to M as soon as I can. I in the meantime, Mrs Watson, I would strongly urge that you not go looking for this village. You would only be looking for trouble."

"My dear Mr….what is your name?"

"Granger, ma'am."

"Mr Granger, I am afraid I have no choice. I cannot stand by and do nothing while something terrible may be happening to my maid."

"Mrs Watson, I really must—"

"No, Mr Granger, my mind is made up. Thank you for your to help. Good bye." I replaced the receiver into the cradle and vowed not to answer the telephone if it rang again.

"Mrs Watson," a voice from behind me called, and I turned to see Mr McCrory entering the room. "Were you on the telephone just now? I hope you were not contacting Scotland Yard."

"I was not. I was, erm, trying to call the station to confirm the train's departure time, given that our Bradshaw edition is rather old, but I was not able to get through. We shall have to take our chances." Lying, I have discovered, only comes easily to me when there is a great deal at stake.

With no time for breakfast, despite my hunger, I pinned a hat over my somewhat dishevelled hair, and we set out for Kings Cross station. Once there, I secured our tickets and boarded the train and after settling into our compartment I attempted to calm myself, rationalizing that there was nothing more I could do for Missy other than what I was doing, and that her fate was now as much in the hands of the engineer's as mine. It was not a successful argument, though, and I knew that every second spent until I saw for myself that the girl was safe would be fraught with anxiety. As for Mr Mc-Crory, it was impossible to tell if he was similarly suffering from fear, since no sooner had we escaped the confines of London for the countryside he fell into a deep, loud slumber.

Since there was nothing else I could do during the hours it would take us to get to Yorkshire, I pulled out the Bradshaw and began perusing it, wishing I had brought a proper book. But upon realizing that I only charted the journey from London to Kingston-upon-Hull earlier this morning, I rechecked the timetable to see what lay beyond. It was with a feeling of triumph mixed with apprehension that I saw there was indeed a station listed for Clytendom Odd located twenty-three minutes' distance from another village called Wandsea, confirming that the place had actually been there as late as 1902. But how does one eradicate an entire village and all traces of it in a mere four years? Or, if Mr McCrory was to be believed, one year?

Given that the writing of Mr Bradshaw not quite being up to that of Mr Dickens or Mr Collins, I confess to having nodded off, the book still in my hands, only to be awakened by the conductor just shy of Doncaster, where we had to make a transfer to Kingston-upon-Hull. Attempting to stifle a yawn as I stepped onto the platform, I hoped that we would not be delayed. Fortunately, the train that would continue our journey arrived within the quarter-hour.

"I apologize for dozing," Mr McCrory said as we boarded the second train, "it was quite inconsiderate of me."

"I slept as well, I'm afraid," I said, "even without having been abducted and—" Suddenly I stopped speaking, having noticed another passenger, a smallish man with a bowler hat and a long coat. I would not have paid any particular attention to the fellow except for the fact that I had seen him on the train from London as well. "That man over there, the one in the bowler, he is not, by any chance, one of your abductors, is he?"

Mr McCrory studied the fellow. "No, he is far too small. Why would you even think so?"

I did not immediately reply, but instead proceeded to our new seats, this carriage being too small to accommodate compartments. Once seated, I whispered: "I saw that man in the bowler hat on the train from London."

"Mrs Watson, surely we are not the only people travelling from London to Yorkshire."

"No, of course we are not," I said. But neither could I shake the impression that the man was trying his utmost not to be caught watching us.

Upon arriving in Hull, we once again had to transfer, this time to a carriage that was even smaller and less patronized. Before long, the fusty, snowy-haired conductor appeared to tell us that the station for the village of Wandsea was approaching. "That is nice," I said, "but we are going to Clytendom Odd."

"Are you certain you are on the right line?" the old fellow asked.

"Yes, why?"

"Because all that is beyond Wandsea is the end of the line."

"There is a station beyond Wandsea," Mr McCrory said, "and please do not try to tell me there isn't, because I have seen it."

"Oh, there's a station, all right, but it's no longer used."

"So you're saying we cannot take the train to the end of the line?"

"I'm saying unless you like watching an engine spin around like a clock hand in a roundhouse there's no reason not to get off at Wandsea."

"In that case, we'll get off at Wandsea," I said. "Oh, and did you happen to see two large men and a young lady on the earlier train?"

"Well, there were a lot of men, some of them large, and a lot of ladies, some of them young. That's the best I can tell you."

"Thank you, sir." The conductor touched his hat brim, smiled, and walked away.

When he was gone, Mr McCrory said, "Mrs Watson, we cannot get off at Wandsea. What if the men and Missy have made their way to Clytendom Odd?"

"I said we would get off there. I did not say we would stay there."

When the train came to a halt we dutifully deboarded onto the platform with the few other passengers. The railway clock proclaimed it to be 11:41, which was remarkably close to the time noted in the four-year-old Bradshaw. Once inside the tiny station, I said, loudly enough to be heard by all, "Oh, heavens, I left something on board," and raced back out. Mr McCrory followed me, and within seconds we were back on the train. "The carriage behind us is the baggage wagon," I whispered to him, "we can hide in there." Making our way to the baggage wagon, which offered many shadows and places in which to hide, we sequestered ourselves until the train once more left the station heaving for... well, we would soon discover where.

"I don't think we need to stay hidden any more," Mr McCrory said, rising from the shadows. "I think we're the only people on board."

"I suspect you are right," I told him, similarly emerging the cover. "That does raise a rather interesting question, though."

"What?"

"If only the two of us are travelling to the end of the line, whose baggage is all of this?"

A silhouette then appeared in the doorway of the carriage, and both Mr McCrory and I crouched back down. The door opened and the man in the bowler hat entered, looked around, and then exited again. When he was gone I said, "Something very odd is going on here."

"You don't have to convince me of that, Mrs Watson."

Some minutes later the train began to decelerate. "Our stop," Mr McCrory said. Yet something was wrong. I pulled the Bradshaw out of my bag and re-examined the page listing the schedule to Clytendom Odd.

"This cannot be correct," I said. "We cannot have been squirreled away in this car for twenty-three minutes. Please check your watch, would you?"

Mr McCrory pulled out his elegant pocketwatch, opened it and said, "It is eleven-fifty-seven."

"Are you certain?"

"Mr Watson, this timepiece was made by A. Lange & Söhne, the finest watchmaker in Germany. If it says eleven-fifty-seven… now fifty-eight…you can bank on it."

"Only sixteen minutes since we pulled into the Wandsea station. I don't understand…" I stopped, having suddenly realized how the village of Clytendom Odd could have disappeared so thoroughly. "Oh, heavens, I do understand. It is so simple and yet it is not. But it is the only possible explanation. Yet it solves very little."

"What are you talking about?" Mr McCrory said.

"According to the railway guide, it should have taken twenty-three minutes to get to Clytendom Odd from Wandsea, yet the actual time was closer to sixteen minutes, even less when you consider that we were stopped at the Wandsea station for a while."

"But what does that mean?"

"It means that Clytendom Odd is another nine or so minutes up the line, and that this station and the roundhouse are shams."

Benedict McCrory's mouth dropped open. "In god's name," he asked, "for what purpose?"

"I cannot imagine, but at the moment it matters less than rescuing Missy from those two brutes. Come along." Stepping back into the empty passenger carriage, I saw the small, seemingly forsaken station coming into view through the window. "We must hurry if we wish to get off," I said, but Mr McCrory was already standing by the door facing away from the station.

"The coast appears to be clear," he announced, carefully opening the door, through which we stepped out and onto rail bed. Using the train to obscure our movements, we made our way to the roundhouse, which certainly looked real, stopping only when we heard voices from the other side of the train, which I took to be those of the conductor and engineer. "Proceed as quietly as possible," I told my cohort. We made it to the side of the roundhouse just as its great doors were opening to allow in the engine.

"It is unbelievable that this roundhouse and that station are merely *doppelgängers*," Mr McCrory said. "Who would do such a thing?"

Who indeed? I thought, *and why indeed*?

We continued to creep around the side of the building, and as we did, I heard Mr McCrory gasp. "Look!" he said, pointing out what I already surmised: railroad tracks on the other side of the roundhouse continued off into the distance, tracks that were obscured by the enormous roundhouse which sat atop them. "Shall we follow them?" he asked.

While I had little doubt that doing so would provide us with the answer to this puzzling matter, I had not really dressed or prepared for a nine mile hike along railroad tracks. As I was attempting to figure out our next move, a great noise sounded behind us. Turning, I saw that the back of the roundhouse was opening. "This way!" I hissed and Mr McCrory followed me back around the side of the building. Moments later, the engine re-emerged with the baggage wagon still attached. "Now we know where the baggage we saw is heading," I whispered. "It's going to Clytendom Odd."

"Once it clears the door, we can jump on at the back of the carriage," Mr McCrory said.

"Young man, I am not a circus daredevil," I replied.

"I suggest you become one," he said, grabbing me by the arm and dragging me to the tracks, pulling me toward the slowly moving train.

"What are you—?" was all I was able to get out before he jumped onto the platform steps in the back and then practically lifted me up to join him. "What on earth do you think you are doing?" I demanded.

"I have to get to Clytendom Odd. Everything depends upon it."

"I wish you had been this forceful and determined against those two men who…oh, oh no. Oh, dear god." Why had I not realized this before? Mr McCrory's characteristic loquaciousness suddenly became relevant to me. In my youth, I had been a member of the Laurence Delancey Players, an amateur theatrics company, and I well recall the voice of old Mr Delancey saying, *My dears, remember, there are only two kinds of people who offer you too much information without your having asked: actors and liars. But to be accomplished as the first, you must never let the audience see you as the second.*

At every opportunity, Benedict McCrory offered too much information.

Turning to him, I said, "Those buildings back there are not the only shams, are they? I have just realized, you have lied to me at every turn. You are in league with whoever has Missy, aren't you?"

He smiled and in that moment his entire demeanour changed. His features were the same, though they were now seemingly constructed of a different, harder material. "How clever you are, for a *fräulein*," he said. "Wrong, of course, but clever. You see, there are no abductors. They are the stuff of fiction, as was everything I have told you, the map, the diary, the old man, the photography, even the fact that I have ever set foot in Clytendom Odd. Everything has been a story."

"Missy's disappearance is not a story."

"Your stupid maid is perfectly safe and probably back in your house by now, after having spent the night with *Fräu* Hudson. It seems the girl is in love with me, which means she might be useful to me in the future. And she is not unattractive, even if she does have the brain of a sheep."

Fräu Hudson; *fräulein, doppelgänger*; his German-made watch. "You are from the Wilhelmstrasse, aren't you?" I asked.

He nodded in a bow and then pulled from his pocket a strange-looking gun, which he pointed at me. "A man from the Wilhelmstrasse complete with a fine German-made pistol called a Luger, which he will use if you make a move to escape," he said.

"Your English is excellent."

"Of course."

"Though in retrospect the fact that you appeared not to know what a Bradshaw was should have told me that you were not an Englishman."

"A minor slip. Thank you for pointing it out."

"What in heaven's name is this game about?"

"The future, Mrs Watson. Nothing less than the future."

"I do not understand."

"We are going to finish the journey. We are going to go to Clytendom Odd."

"Why?"

"Be still. You ask too many questions."

I remained silent as I quickly weighed my options and equally quickly realized I had none that were viable. My only solace was that Missy was safe, if this horrible man was finally telling the truth, though I feared her heart was destined for another shattering. Before long the train began slowing again and the station came into view through the window.

"Come," he said, pushing the gun into my side and forcing me toward the back of the car and onto the platform.

"You don't expect me to jump while the train is in motion, do you?" I asked.

"It is slowing," he replied. "If you would rather not jump, I can shoot you now and let your body fall onto the tracks, but after all we have been through, I would so hate to have to do that."

When the train was nearly at a halt, I jumped, and fortunately did not turn my ankle upon landing. Benedict McCrory, or whatever his name really was, jumped after me. Once more grabbing my arm, he roughly pulled me toward the station building, from whence I saw two workmen emerge and walk to the train, entering it through the baggage carriage, too occupied with their tasks to notice that we were even near. I quickly considered shouting out to them but did not wish to have my cry immediately followed by a gunshot. Once the men were fully engaged in their duties, the German ran me around to the back of the building where sat a lorry and team, presumably there to transport the baggage into the village. "Come on," he said, practically shoving me up into the lorry and then leaping up beside me. Taking the reins in one hand, and holding the pistol on me with the other, he reined the horses into action and we sped down the rutted road, bouncing almost uncontrollably, moving far too fast for me to attempt to jump out.

"If you are really intent upon killing me, why haven't you done so?" I asked, shouting over the sounds of the racing cart.

"We have not yet reached the destination," he replied. "I still may need you."

"At least, tell me what this is all about. You owe me that much."

"Very well. It is quite simple, really. My government learned that a small, inconsequential village called Clytendom Odd had been commandeered by your government and made into the site of an elite military training facility, one whose soldiers are to be used as agents working against foreign powers. There is a conflict coming, Mrs Watson, mark my words, and in that conflict, we intend to be victorious. So it was decided that such a facility could not be allowed to operate. It has to be either infiltrated or destroyed. That was my assignment. Yet when I came here and attempted to locate such a village, I found, too, that it seemed to have vanished off the face of the earth. I knew that some form of chicanery was behind it and rationalized that the quickest way to discover the truth was to engage Sherlock Holmes."

"Whom you assumed would not have seen through you."

"I did assume so, yes. From the reports we have obtained of Holmes, once the puzzle had been lain before him, he is blind to all but the puzzle itself."

"He is a more ingenious man than your reports have made so," I said. While I may have had my problems with my distant cousin, I was not about to let this German brute besmirch him.

"Perhaps, perhaps not, but that was ultimately made redundant by his unavailability. So I was led to you. Quite frankly, I was sceptical that you would be of any help until I met you, at which time I decided that perhaps *Fräu* Hudson had known whereof she spoke regarding your skills. But I was not expecting that you would initially turn me down, which was when I had to elaborate upon my plans. During my evening out with your maid, I asked her many questions about you, chiefly what she thought it would take to get you to reconsider taking my case. She told me that you invariably rushed into the breach to help those to whom you were close. So, in order to coerce you into helping, I made it appear that someone close to you, your maid, was in danger. The stupid girl was so taken with me that she readily agreed to the ruse and offered to hide out for a day in Baker Street in order to support the story that she had been abducted. The plan was really quite ingenious, when you think about it, particularly for one concocted on such short notice."

"Shall I slide over to provide more room for your opinion of yourself?" I asked.

"You shall not move one jot," he said, pressing the gun deeper into my side.

Ahead of us, the first outlines of buildings were coming into view. We continued to gallop dangerously until we were within the deserted centre of Clytendom Odd, at which point he reined the horses to a halt. "All right, get down," he commanded and I did. "You look frightened, Mrs Watson. A resourceful person like you, frightened. Why is that?"

He appeared to be enjoying this, so much so that it gave me an idea: while I am not so foolish as to claim that I was *not* frightened, the Hunnish brute was taking so much pleasure at the thought of my fear that I decided to play into his cruel need to terrorize me, hoping it would provide additional time to think of a way to extricate myself from this situation. Shrinking back in melodramatic fashion, I stared at the pistol with widened eyes and gasped: "Please…please, Mr McCrory, or whoever you are, please don't kill me." My performance was proving effective, since his smile broadened.

"I wonder where I shall shoot you first?" he said.

"No, I beg of you!" I cried, throwing one hand to my forehead and reaching out to him with the other. "Is there is no way I can entreat you to spare my life?"

"I'm afraid not, though I will endeavour to make it quick."

I knew that this was the time to act. "Oh, I feel faint…" I moaned, moving my hand to the top of my hat and weaving back and forth. He tightened his grip on the Luger. With as much force as I could muster, I toppled into him while extracting from my hat my long jewelled hatpin. Given the element of surprise, abetted by the fact that I am not a tiny woman, he was not prepared to catch me, which was my plan. With a startled cry he went down, my entire weight falling on top of him. Before he could react, I took my hatpin and jabbed it into the wrist of his hand that held the pistol. With another cry, he let loose of the gun, which I retrieved while he struggled to remove the pin from his bleeding wrist.

"Now it is your turn to remain still," I said, training the Luger on him. I have never shot a man and in truth had precious little experience even holding a firearm. But since I was still playing a role, I did my best not to reveal that.

"Is this how it ends?" he asked. "I am to be outdone by a mere woman?"

"Might want to get used to it, chappy," a voice suddenly said behind me. Startled, I turned to look; it was the man I had seen on the train, the one in the bowler who appeared to be watching us, who was now holding a rifle in his hands. "A word of advice, ma'am," he said, "never turn your back on a suspect, even if you do have the gun."

"But which of you is the suspect?" I cried.

"He is," the man said. "This is Baron Alexander von Neuss, one the Germany Imperial Army's best undercover men. When you mentioned that Heidelberg scar over the telephone, I knew immediately who you were dealing with."

"You are Mr Granger?"

"Yes'm, and you can put that Luger down now."

Now more armed men appeared, seemingly out of thin air, all surrounding Baron von Neuss, who remained on the ground, shouting a string of words in German, whose meanings I suspect I did not wish to know. Within seconds the soldiers restrained him, pulled him to his feet and escorted him into one of the buildings (where I hoped one of them would think to extract my hatpin and return it to me). When they were gone I asked Mr Granger, "You followed us from London, didn't you?"

"Aye, on orders. I was hoping to apprehend von Neuss at the station but he proved too quick in escaping. You handled yourself like a real professional, Mrs Watson."

"I am *not* a professional!"

"Right. About that, if you would be so good as to come with me?" He extended his arm in courtly fashion and led me to the village pub, whose sign proclaimed it The Prince of Whales.

"Isn't that sign misspelled?" I asked.

The man smiled. "It is a jest, one that was provided by His Majesty King Edward himself."

Upon entering, I saw that it was not a pub at all but rather an office of some sort, but with a decided club atmosphere. A perfect place for *The Prince of Whales*. "I know you are here, Mycroft," I said, acknowledging that only he had the wherewithal to make an entire village disappear. "Please present yourself."

"Hello, my dear," said a very familiar voice, and turning to it I saw the enormous, lugubrious figure of my distant relative moving toward me, with the speed of a glacier. "I am happy to see you, Amelia."

"I am certainly not unhappy to see you," I replied, "though I confess that I had a few bad moments out there."

"Which you handled admirably. Please, sit down," he said, directing me to a table. "Wine?"

"Thank you, I believe I shall."

With a mere look at Mr Granger, he ordered glasses of red wine for both of us, which were of a quality I had never before experienced. "You were never in any real danger, Amelia," Mycroft told me.

"It certainly felt like I was."

"Even so, we had snipers with the Baron in their crosshairs from every vantage point. Were he to make any suspicious move, we would have brought the situation to a conclusion."

I sipped the wine, which was more than excellent, it was superb. "You do not consider a man pointing a gun at someone to be a suspicious move?"

"With time, you will learn what truly constitutes danger and what is merely the preamble." He took a sip of his own wine.

"What do you mean, 'with time?' Oh, Mycroft, you are not talking about that offer you made me?"

"I must tell you the last thing I expected to hear yesterday was a report from my man that you telephoned regarding Clytendom Odd. We received intelligence that Baron von Neuss was in the country and was likely attempting to find a way to infiltrate our little compound here. But when I heard that you were involved on behalf of a client whose description matched his rather nicely, well, I felt the hand of providence nearby."

"May I have some more of this wine?" I asked, and my glass was immediately refilled. "You know, Mycroft, I have been largely in the dark throughout this entire affair. I was taken in by a list of lies longer than *Bleak House*, which is hardly the requirement for a first class spy."

"On the contrary, Amelia, you were held at gunpoint by a trained assassin and yet here you are sitting with me sipping wine while he is being held in captivity. You engineered your own survival, and survival, my dear, is a requirement for a first class spy. Though I do dislike that word."

"Survival?"

"No, spy."

"So this village is not a university for spies?"

He set down his glass. "Let us say instead a facility for training operatives hidden from the eyes of the world. At least we thought so. Clytendom Odd was one of a half-dozen villages that were dying on the vine. The last resident abandoned it more than two years ago, leaving it a quickly forgotten ghost village and therefore perfect for our purposes. Naturally, in order to secure the premises, hide them from the eyes of the world, as it were, we had to make it 'vanish.' It took some doing but we thought we had been successful until we found out that our German counterparts had somehow learned of the name Clytendom Odd. Because of that, I am afraid we shall have to relocate, which is an inconvenience of the first magnitude, given the expense to which we have gone to eradicate this village. I can assure you that building a folly round-house does not come cheaply. You may have faced a German pistol, but I now have to face the Home Secretary."

After another sip of wine, I asked: "What will happen to the Baron? Will he take up residence in the Tower?"

"Worse," Mycroft said, "he will spend the rest of his days in Australia where we still maintain prisons, unless a better use for him emerges at some point. But enough of our German friend. What of you, cousin? Will you join M Division? The way you handled yourself in this matter was most impressive and there are situations in which we need a woman's touch."

"Mycroft, really—"

"Amelia, His Majesty needs you. I need you."

"But John needs me, too."

"I am certain that we can come to an agreement with the good doctor."

Oh, dear god! I closed my eyes and took a deep breath and gave him my answer.

Holding his glass out for another refill, Mycroft continued to talk to me but I was not listening. Instead I was thinking about how I was going to explain to John when he returned from America that I was henceforth in the employ of His Majesty's government as a spy through M Division.

How could I explain it to myself?

Michael Mallory is a writer on animation and post-war pop culture. Mallory also writes murder mysteries, often featuring "Amelia Watson," the second (and previously unheralded) wife of Dr Watson of Sherlock Holmes fame. Four volumes of Amelia Watson stories have appeared to date: *The Adventures of the Second Mrs. Watson, Murder in the Bath, The Exploits of the Second Mrs. Watson,* and *The Stratford Conspiracy.*

WHEN STARS COLLIDE

by BV Lawson

He had to admit the corpse looked quite lifelike in that sacque suit, the presentation complete except for the missing bowler hat. Too bad. Baber had loved his bowler hats. Shapley peered down at the casket to get a better look and was startled to see faint dark patches on Baber's face. Definitely not day-old whiskers. But what else could it be?

Harlow Shapley turned to study his fellow mourners, realizing how few of them were ever up as early as ten in the morning. "Vampires, that's what we are," he muttered to himself. Why were astronomers never the stars of vampire stories, seeing as how they shunned the sunlight just as completely? Maybe Gustave le Rouge got it right with his tale of bat-winged, blood-drinking humanoids on Mars. What an astronomical discovery *that* would be.

Shapley suspected his colleagues felt the same way he did— sorry about Baber's unfortunate accident, but chafing at how the fuss took time away from their telescopes. Except maybe Hubble. Shapley saw the man out of the corner of his eye, chatting up all the single women in the room, as usual. At least on this occasion Hubble traded his standard Oxford getup of jodhpurs and high-topped military boots in favor of a more conservative American suit.

After paying his respects to Baber's fiancée, Rachel, Shapley made a beeline to a short man with fiery red hair he'd seen earlier who'd been hovering around the room for the entire viewing. "Are you the mortician?"

"Yes, yes, I am," the man nodded.

"The strange dark spots on the deceased's face. Can you tell me anything about those?"

The mortician's own face was cratered like the moon from pox scars, made worse when he wrinkled his brow. "I tried my best. The bruises were so bad, the makeup couldn't cover them. You think the family noticed?" He looked around and lowered his voice, "My credentials are impeccable, I assure you, but business has been down since the war and sometimes you have to make do."

Shapley patted him on the shoulder. "Of course. I understand." But his mind wasn't on the mortician's problems. He was trying to figure out how a man like Baber who'd allegedly fallen straight off a cliff onto his back, as the police said, would have gotten facial bruises.

The more he considered it, the more Shapley's journalistic sixth sense tingled. One thing he'd learned from working the crime beat at the *Joplin Times*, you never took inconsistencies for granted.

Shapley tried to tackle his normal business the rest of the day, but his usual daydreams of Cepheid variables ended up morphing into yellow-purplish bruises on a giant cosmic face. That night, driving his pride-and-joy 1920 Nash Roadster up the twisting road to Mount Wilson in the darkness of the new moon was more dangerous than usual with fresh snow banks. But it did help take his mind off Baber. So much so, that when he arrived at the top of the mountain, he was ready to charge over to the 60-inch telescope.

Almost ready.

He felt himself being pulled as if by an invisible magnet to the cliff drop-off outside the "Monastery," the astronomers' living quarters. He hadn't visited the spot where Baber's body was found, but he knew where it was, right below that drop-off. Whipping out a flashlight, he picked his way down a path the emergency crew carved to the ledge where Baber fell three nights ago.

With no snowfall since, Shapley could still see the outlines of where the body came to rest, as well as a set of footprints that weren't Shapley's, large ones, like a boot would make. Those must belong to the medical worker who'd attended to Baber.

As Shapley trained his flashlight around the ledge, he noticed something else, a clump of tobacco. But Baber wasn't a smoker, and Shapley doubted the medic would take time for a pipe in an emergency. He picked up a few strands and took a whiff. Smelled a lot like that Tuxedo stuff Hubble used. He wadded the strands into a vest pocket.

Turning the flashlight away from the footprints, he got an unshakeable impression something wasn't right. He bent down close to the ground, and from that vantage point, he could see what was hard to spy from above—the snow had intentionally been brushed with something. But why?

He bent over further until his face touched the snow. He spied the faint remnant of a shoe tread. Unlike the bootprints he thought were the medic's, this tread was smooth with an Oxford-style heel. Just a few feet away, a Manzanita branch lay with one end as smooth as if cut by a knife.

So. The bruises on Baber's face made sense if someone hit him before he fell. And it made equal sense such an attacker would check if Baber was alive or dead, then cover up his tracks with the Manzanita branch. After discovering Hubble's favorite brand of tobacco at the scene, Shapely couldn't help but suspect the six-foot-three astronomer—a former star athlete and heavyweight boxer.

His curiosity fully aroused, Shapley headed back to the Monastery toward Baber's former room, surprised to find no one thought to gather Baber's belongings and give them to his family. He started searching. He should feel guilty, but he didn't.

It only took a few minutes to look through Baber's meager possessions—a few clothes, a shaving mug with safety razor and a tin can of Williams shaving powder, plus a couple of books including a Zane Grey western and a book of Sherlock Holmes stories. Ah, Holmes. Sherlock Holmes didn't like inconsistencies, either. So what would the Master Detective do next?

Glancing around, it was easy to see there were no hiding places, except perhaps the mattress. Shapley lifted up the head of the bed and felt around, just to be sure. Nothing but sheets. When he lifted up the foot of the bed, his hand fell on something hard, and he pulled out a package wrapped in brown paper with a series of figures scribbled on top.

His fingers shook as he peeled away the paper to reveal an astronomical plate. Not just any plate—Shapley could tell it was one of ten missing photographic plates stolen from his own room a few weeks ago.

Anger and the hurt of betrayal threatened to overwhelm him, but he forced those feelings aside. His scientific and journalistic discipline kicked in as he considered those missing plates, which vanished when he left them in his room only long enough to get a carrying case from the Nash.

The plates were a series he took that could lead to a break-through in his work. They might even be crucial for the upcoming debate with Heber Curtis from the Lick Observatory, proving Curtis was wrong and Shapley was right—a distant spiral nebulae did lie within the Milky Way galaxy. Shapley returned the plate to its hiding place under the mattress, but he tucked the brown paper wrapper inside his coat.

Switching on the red bulb in his Franco three-in-one flashlight, he stumbled his way to the sixty-inch observatory. His assistant, Carl Quillen, had already opened the dome and was engaging the clock-drive mechanism before mounting the ladder up to the eye-piece.

As Shapley entered, Quillen said, "There's a tragic face. What happened? Did Martha find an error in your calculations again? You know she's better at math than you are."

Yes, Shapley knew. His wife was better at a lot of things than he was and helped him out with his research more times than he could remember. "No, that's not it. Not this time, anyway. It's Baber."

Quillen climbed the ladder and perched on the platform against the railing. "Baber? What about him?"

"I don't think his death was an accident."

"You mean suicide? He was Catholic, you know."

"No, not suicide. I found some things at the site where he fell."

"Like what?"

"Tobacco for one. Smells a lot like Tuxedo. Then there was a patch of snow that looked like someone was covering up his tracks. And that's not all."

"Okay, I'll bite. What else?"

"There were bruises on Baber's face at the viewing. Why would he have bruises if he fell on his back? It doesn't add up. I think the whole thing has something to do with my stolen plates."

"Yeah? That was rather odd. I mean, why steal photographic plates? Unless it's Pierson. He left the Lick Observatory under a big cloud of mystery. I overheard him say he'd do anything to get back in the good graces of the astronomical community. 'Anything' might just include theft. Maybe he's a spy for the Lick."

Shapley stamped his feet on the floor, more to fend off the cold than out of frustration. "I think you've still got the war mentality. Spying? Pierson isn't German."

"Neither's Hubble, but he was in the war, too. As if we could forget, telling everyone he wanted to be addressed as 'Major Hubble, if you please' when he returned. Although I'd lay wagers he never got near the Ardennes."

Shapley laughed. "Those Hollywood types he's hobnobbing with don't help matters. He probably thinks he'll go down in history as the world's most famous astronomer, have some giant observatory named after him while everyone else is forgotten."

"But you said it was his tobacco brand you found?"

Shapley sobered up quickly. "Yeah. Say, Carl, you were the one to find Baber's body. You told the authorities you didn't see any bruises. Is that right?"

"I was kinda in shock, to tell the truth. I saw him lying there on his back, then ran to get help."

"So you didn't climb down to check on him?"

Quillen positioned himself in front of the eyepiece. "I couldn't tell how far a drop it was in the dark. Didn't think I could help poor Baber by tumbling down on top of him."

"You had your flashlight, didn't you?"

"Those dim red lights are barely good enough to keep me from tripping over my own feet." Quillen slid into place in his seat, placing one hand to the side of the guide scope pointed at a reference star that he'd use to nudge the sixty-inch during the exposure to keep it precisely aimed, then grabbed the controls of the plate shutter with the other hand.

"Did you know Baber well, Carl?"

"He was near penniless and desperate for cash. He'd taken a second day job at a factory and rarely got any sleep, napping in one-hour shifts when he could. But that's it."

"What about his fiancée, Rachel Oberlin?" In the isolated environment of Mount Wilson with its close quarters, rumors were a primary form of entertainment. One or two hinted at an argument over Rachel between Carl Quillen and Baber.

"Nice girl. Too good for him. She's young, though. She'll bounce back." Quillen turned back to the telescope. "Gotta stop talking now or I'll fog up the eyepiece."

Feeling a little like he'd been dismissed, Shapley decided to get some air outside. He headed out along the footbridge across the arroyo leading to the hundred-inch telescope, Hubble's baby, but stopped when he thought he saw movement ahead.

In the red beam from Shapley's flashlight, he could just make out the eerie silhouette of Delano Pierson smoking a pipe. Approaching him cautiously so as not to startle him, he called out softly, "Hey, Del, that you?"

The figure turned to face him, smoke rings glinting in the red light as they rose into the air. "You're out early, aren't you, Harlow?" Pierson's drawl gave every word an extra syllable, contrasting with Quillen's rapid-fire delivery. When Shapley was between the two, he always felt like a translator.

"Carl's prepping the 'scope as we speak, but frankly, I can't concentrate on Cepheids right now."

"Must be something interesting to drag the famous Harlow Shapley's attention away from his Cepheid variables. Is it Martha? The kids?"

"No, no, they're fine. As I was saying to Carl, I think Baber's death was intentional. As in murder."

Pierson blew more smoke rings into an ascending pyramid of concentric circles. "Murder, you say. A bit extreme. What's the motive?"

"Theft, blackmail, maybe. Baber was having financial troubles. And I found one of my missing plates under his mattress."

"I suppose someone who's gotten engaged and needs to support a family with no money might get desperate. But he couldn't have murdered himself. So if I follow your logic, somebody else was involved. Got anyone in mind?"

"Can't imagine any of us doing the deed. Hardly sporting, is it?"

"People can surprise you. Hide their true colors, all dressed up in their proper black and whites. Take your assistant, Carl Quillen, for example. He's incredibly insecure, but he covers it up with bravado."

"I never noticed. Why would he be insecure?"

"His humble beginnings. From farm to Mount Wilson janitor to astronomer. That's quite a leap. He's not a privileged Oxford elite like Hubble."

Shapley knew of such things first-hand, seeing as how his own father was a farmer and Shapley attended a one-room school. "True, but he seems confident to me."

"Seems, yes. You know George Hale's planning a bigger observatory, the largest telescope in the world, over on Palomar? Quillen wants to get in Hale's good graces and be hired there one day. If you want to discuss motive, perhaps Quillen wanted those plates of yours. He could subvert your research, make you look bad in front of Hale. Then he'd be the one who comes to the rescue with the correct data. What was on those plates, anyway?'

"They were from a promising night of observations. I needed that data to verify I was on the right track about the size of the Milky Way."

"Hmm." Pierson tapped his pipe on the railing of the footbridge. "Come to think of it, I remember Baber saying he was going to meet someone the night he died. That was three days ago, yes?"

"Yes. But did he say who?"

"Can't recall. Maybe the same person who gave him that wad of cash."

"What wad of cash, Del? I thought he was broke."

"I saw him pull it out of his wallet not long ago. I figured he'd gotten an advance or some such thing. But if he was off selling your plates, well…"

Shapley gazed up at the dome housing the hundred-inch telescope. What was Hubble doing with *his* evening? Definitely not playing a two-bit Sherlock Holmes. That would be beneath him. "I see you're smoking your pipe there, Del. You use Tuxedo?"

"Tuxedo? That's Hubble's brand. I'm a frequent traveler of the Lucky Strike trail, myself."

"That so?" Shapley smiled. He avoided that narrow rocky trail like a plague, even though it was a shortcut across the plunging slope from the Observatory to the so-called Mount Wilson Hotel and its tobacco stand. You'd have to be a true addict to risk it.

So Pierson used Lucky Strike, not Hubble's Tuxedo brand. But it suddenly occurred to Shapley that Hubble often kept the door to his Monastery room open, his tin of tobacco on a table. Anyone could have ducked in there and taken some, just as they did Shapley's plates. Pierson himself could have planted the tobacco where Baber fell to lead suspicion in Hubble's direction.

Or Pierson might be lying about Baber meeting someone the night he was killed.

"Tell me, Del. How well did you know Baber? He'd been here, what—six months?"

"Five. I tried to get to know the kid, but he kept things close to his vest. I doubt Carl Quillen tried to get to know him. They were romantic rivals, from what I hear, over Rachel Oberlin. She had a small inheritance, though no self-respecting man would be content to live off his wife's income. Still, both Baber and Quillen could have used that money of hers."

Shapley glanced up in time to catch sight of a meteor as it ablated through the atmosphere. He normally focused through an eyepiece on pinpoints of light thousands of parsecs away and often forgot to just gaze up at the bejeweled sky. A sky he knew was far larger than ever thought before, with Earth's lowly sun on the outer fringes of the galaxy.

Astronomy had a way of humbling its practitioners. Or at least, it should. Hubble's ego seemed to get bigger the farther out he looked.

"And you, Del? Are you insecure, too, like our poor unfortunate Baber? And, as you say, Carl Quillen?"

"Insecure? No. Depressed? Hell, yes. Life has a funny way of collapsing in on itself. That's why I need this job, Harlow."

Recalling Quillen's comments minutes earlier about Del and the mysterious departure from his previous job, Shapley asked, "What for? Absolution? Redemption?"

"More like obsession. The only peace I have is when I look at the stars. Astronomy's been my dream since I was a small boy and first got my hands on a Messier catalog of astronomical objects. I can't live without them, those stars."

Del Pierson studied his glowing radium watch. "Alas, that's it. My last pipe for a while. Time to head back and prepare for interferometer measurements. If Hubble doesn't hog the hundred-inch 'scope all night."

Shapley watched Pierson fade into the darkness. As he touched his pocket, he felt the crinkling of the brown paper wrapper from the photographic plate in Baber's room. Studying the figures on the paper now with his flashlight, he noticed patterns he'd missed when he let his anger overrule his common sense. Like focusing a fuzzy light through a 'scope, he realized what the figures were, if not what they stood for. Changing course, he turned around and headed for the larger of the two domes.

Edwin Hubble, dressed now in his more customary jodhpurs, boots, and English driving cap, was high up in the prime focus cage that resembled the gondola of a hot air balloon, his face illuminated by crimson instrument lights. Shapley hopped in the elevator up to the platform. He hardly ever exchanged two words with Hubble, and he wasn't looking forward to this meeting.

At least he had the satisfaction of seeing the shock on Hubble's face as Shapley drew nearer. "What the devil are you doing here?" the Great One yelled at him. "Can't you see I'm in the middle of my work?"

Shapley pointed to his own face. "Two eyes that work very well, thank you. Yes, I can see that. I need you to answer a couple of questions for me."

"It had better be important, Shapley."

"Oh, I think it is. Nothing short of murder."

"Murder?" Hubble squinted at him. "Have you been drinking?"

"Baber's murder. It wasn't an accident. And he was the one who stole my photographic plates."

"That's nonsense. You must have misplaced those."

"I found one wrapped up and hidden under Baber's mattress. I think he was acting on behalf of someone else."

"I suppose you think that someone was me? Stealing your little plates like some petty thief?"

"Tell me this. The night of Baber's death, you ate at the home of Earl and Grace Leib, as I recall. I only remember it because you were telling everyone within earshot that day. But late that night, I heard someone retching in the Monastery while I was on my break. Did the fancy Leib haute cuisine not sit well with you?"

"If you're asking in your roundabout way if that was me you heard, it was. That *pâté de fois gras*. I was in and out of the bathroom, finally gave up, and left the mountain in search of a doctor. Wasted my entire window for observation."

"As I suspected, that effectively rules you out as our culprit." Shapley held out the brown paper wrapping. "You were in the Army, Major. Is this Morse Code?"

Hubble glanced at the paper. "Dash dot dash dot. That's a 'C.' And dash dash dot dash, a 'Q.' CQ is the code used by wireless operators for a general call. Where did you get this?"

"This is what one of my missing photographic plates was wrapped in. But I don't think CQ stands for general call in this case. You need to come with me, Hubble."

Hubble looked grim, but to Shapley's surprise, he nodded, and the pair made their way down the elevator in an awkward silence. Shapley corralled the other two on-duty astronomers into the Galley, where he poured everyone some coffee and had them sit at the table.

Sherlock Holmes would have Watson at his side and Inspector Lestrade standing by. Shapely keenly felt his isolation, his hands shaking. He grabbed his cup of coffee and gulped down the hot liquid.

Clearing his throat, he began. "Ordinarily, when we're all together like this, it's to discuss the latest developments in our field or take a meal. But this is no ordinary event, I'm afraid."

Journalism background or no, Shapley wasn't finding this easy. He took several more gulps of coffee, burning his throat. "Fortunately for me, most of our company hasn't returned from the extended Christmas holidays or our list of suspects would be far greater."

Pierson spoke up, "You still think Baber was murdered, Harlow?"

"I do. By one of you. But we can rule out Hubble as he was seeing stars of a different kind, suffering from food poisoning. Our culprit planted some evidence to frame him, namely Hubble's Tuxedo tobacco, but it isn't going to work."

Hubble's face looked stormy, and Shapley expected a thundering tirade, but Hubble stayed silent. Shapley continued, "Delano has motive and opportunity. I know he often smokes his pipe near the area where Baber died. There's always the possibility he's a spy for Lick or acting on his own in stealing those photographic plates. For sabotage, fame or money."

Pierson sputtered and put down his coffee. "Now, see here, Shapley—"

Shapley put up his hand to stop the outburst, took another gulp of the coffee and wished it were something stronger. Too bad alcohol was banned from the mountain. "Carl is the one who found Baber's body with his flashlight. But if you stand on that cliff, it isn't easy to see down, especially in the dark. I asked myself, 'Why would he be looking down specifically there at that exact time?' Then there were the bruises. Carl said he didn't see any bruises on Baber's face, the story he told the authorities. Yet the mortician at the viewing had to use heavy makeup to cover up facial bruises. I also found evidence of a footprint someone tried to obscure with a cut branch. Again, why?"

Pierson leaned forward and propped his head thoughtfully on his chin. "Interesting, Harlow, but it's a weak case."

"So far. But the paper my stolen photographic plate was wrapped in had Morse code for CQ on it, which Hubble here says stands for general call, something all military folks would know. CQ also stands for Carl Quillen."

Shapley tried to ignore his assistant's face, turned as white as the snow piled against the Galley's walls. "Carl served in the war, so he'd know Morse code, something he and Baber could use for their exchanges. He also grew up on a farm, where hunting and tracking are common. It would have been natural for him to cover up his tracks after leaving that tobacco and checking on Baber to make sure he was dead before he called for help. Carl and Baber didn't get along to start with, even fought over the same girl, but they'd formed an uneasy partnership, it's my guess, to steal photographic plates."

Hubble growled, "A fight over a woman I can understand, but plates, Shapley?"

"Carl was ambitious. Desperate to get a spot at the new Palomar Observatory. He knew those plates were important in my research. I suppose he hoped he could use them to trump my discoveries and gain accolades for his own. Although Carl had the easiest access to the plates, he knew Baber was penniless, so he likely bribed him into helping steal and hide the plates. Maybe promised to give up his pursuit of Rachel in return."

Shapley turned toward Carl, the man ramrod straight with arms plastered by his sides. No cries of innocence, no pleas in his own defense. Pierson and Hubble were both staring at Quillen now, their former expressions of disbelief turning to realization. Hubble was the one who got up first, turning around without so much as a backward glance before heading out the door.

Pierson was slower, but also rose out of his chair and walked toward the exit. Before he left, Shapley stopped him. "One moment, Del. Since we're spilling a lot of guts here, why did you really leave the Lick Observatory?"

Pierson sighed and gave a sad smile. "If you must know, my wife was having an affair with the assistant director." With a nod of his head, he disappeared into the night.

Shapley muttered, "We're not an observatory, we're a pulp novel."

Quillen stayed silent, staring down at the table. Shapley asked, "Where are the other plates?"

Quillen didn't answer, and Shapley studied him for moment. "At least tell me this. Was Baber's death an accident or intentional?"

He'd hoped to see cracks in Quillen's stony gaze, a hint of remorse, but there was more life coming out of one of Shapley's pulsing Cepheids. "You were a damned fine assistant, Carl." And with that, Shapley followed the example of the others and exited quietly, going in search of a security guard. Maybe not Inspector Lestrade, but it would have to do. It was out of Shapley's hands.

He should get back on the proverbial horse, or telescope in this case, and continue the work Quillen had set up for the night. That debate with Curtis was only three short months away. He only hoped those missing plates wouldn't come back to haunt him and throw off his calculations. Hubble would love that. A great way for Shapley to "come a cropper" in Hubble's words. Nah, the missing plates wouldn't matter. Curtis was wrong. Those spiral nebulae couldn't possibly lie outside the galaxy. The Milky Way was all there was in the universe. All there would ever be.

✗

A CASE OF IDENTITY

by Sir Arthur Conan Doyle

"**M**y dear fellow," said Sherlock Holmes, as we sat on either side of the fire in his lodgings at Baker Street, "life is infinitely stranger than anything which the mind of man can invent. We would not dare to conceive the things which are really mere commonplaces of existence. If we could fly out of that window hand in hand, hover over this great city, gently remove the roofs, and peep in at the queer things which are going on, the strange coincidences, the plannings, the cross-purposes, the wonderful chains of events, working through generations, and leading to the most *outre* results, it would make all fiction, with its conventionalities and foreseen conclusions, most stale and unprofitable."

"And yet I am not convinced of it," I answered. "The cases which come to light in the papers are, as a rule, bald enough, and vulgar enough. We have in our police reports realism pushed to its extreme limits, and yet the result is, it must be confessed, neither fascinating nor artistic."

"A certain selection and discretion must be used in producing a realistic effect," remarked Holmes. "This is wanting in the police report, where more stress is laid perhaps upon the platitudes of the magistrate than upon the details, which to an observer contain the vital essence of the whole matter. Depend upon it, there is nothing so unnatural as the commonplace."

I smiled and shook my head. "I can quite understand your thinking so," I said. "Of course, in your position of unofficial adviser and helper to everybody who is absolutely puzzled, throughout three continents, you are brought in contact with all that is strange and *bizarre*. But here"—I picked up the morning paper from the ground—"let us put it to a practical test. Here is the first heading upon which I come. 'A husband's cruelty to his wife.' There is half a column of print, but I know without reading it that it is all perfectly familiar to me. There is, of course, the other woman, the drink, the push, the blow, the bruise, the unsympathetic sister or landlady. The crudest of writers could invent nothing more crude."

"Indeed your example is an unfortunate one for your argument," said Holmes, taking the paper, and glancing his eye down it. "This is the Dundas separation case, and, as it happens, I was engaged in clearing up some small points in connection with it. The husband was a teetotaler, there was no other woman, and the conduct complained of was that he had drifted into the habit of winding up every meal by taking out his false teeth and hurling them at his wife, which you will allow is not an action likely to occur to the imagination of the average story teller. Take a pinch of snuff, doctor, and acknowledge that I have scored over you in your example."

He held out his snuffbox of old gold, with a great amethyst in the center of the lid. Its splendor was in such contrast to his homely ways and simple life that I could not help commenting upon it.

"Ah!" said he, "I forgot that I had not seen you for some weeks. It is a little souvenir from the King of Bohemia, in return for my assistance in the case of the Irene Adler papers."

"And the ring?" I asked, glancing at a remarkable brilliant which sparkled upon his finger.

"It was from the reigning family of Holland, though the matter in which I served them was of such delicacy that I cannot confide it even to you, who have been good enough to chronicle one or two of my little problems."

"And have you any on hand just now?" I asked with interest.

"Some ten or twelve, but none which present any features of interest. They are important, you understand, without being interesting. Indeed I have found that it is usually in unimportant matters that there is a field for the observation, and for the quick analysis of cause and effect which gives the charm to an investigation. The larger crimes are apt to be the simpler, for the bigger the crime, the more obvious, as a rule, is the motive. In these cases, save for one rather intricate matter which has been referred to me from Marseilles, there is nothing which presents any features of interest. It is possible, however, that I may have something better before very many minutes are over, for this is one of my clients, or I am much mistaken."

He had risen from his chair, and was standing between the parted blinds, gazing down into the dull, neutral-tinted London street. Looking over his shoulder, I saw that on the pavement opposite there stood a large woman with a heavy fur boa round her neck, and a large curling red feather in a broad-brimmed hat which was tilted in a coquettish Duchess-of-Devonshire fashion over her ear.

From under this great panoply she peeped up in a nervous, hesitating fashion at our windows, while her body oscillated backward and forward, and her fingers fidgeted with her glove buttons. Suddenly, with a plunge, as of the swimmer who leaves the bank, she hurried across the road, and we heard the sharp clang of the bell.

"I have seen those symptoms before," said Holmes, throwing his cigarette into the fire. "Oscillation upon the pavement always means an *affaire de coeur*. She would like advice, but is not sure that the matter is not too delicate for communication. And yet even here we may discriminate. When a woman has been seriously wronged by a man, she no longer oscillates, and the usual symptom is a broken bell wire. Here we may take it that there is a love matter, but that the maiden is not so much angry as perplexed or grieved. But here she comes in person to resolve our doubts."

As he spoke, there was a tap at the door, and the boy in buttons entered to announce Miss Mary Sutherland, while the lady herself loomed behind his small black figure like a full-sailed merchantman behind a tiny pilot boat. Sherlock Holmes welcomed her with the easy courtesy for which he was remarkable, and having closed the door, and bowed her into an armchair, he looked her over in the minute and yet abstracted fashion which was peculiar to him.

"Do you not find," he said, "that with your short sight it is a little trying to do so much typewriting?"

"I did at first," she answered, "but now I know where the letters are without looking." Then, suddenly realizing the full purport of his words, she gave a violent start, and looked up with fear and astonishment upon her broad, good-humored face. "You've heard about me, Mr. Holmes," she cried, "else how could you know all that?"

"Never mind," said Holmes, laughing, "it is my business to know things. Perhaps I have trained myself to see what others overlook. If not, why should you come to consult me?"

"I came to you, sir, because I heard of you from Mrs. Etherege, whose husband you found so easily when the police and everyone had given him up for dead. Oh, Mr. Holmes, I wish you would do as much for me. I'm not rich, but still I have a hundred a year in my own right, besides the little that I make by the machine, and I would give it all to know what has become of Mr. Hosmer Angel."

"Why did you come away to consult me in such a hurry?" asked Sherlock Holmes, with his finger tips together, and his eyes to the ceiling.

Again a startled look came over the somewhat vacuous face of Miss Mary Sutherland. "Yes, I did bang out of the house," she said, "for it made me angry to see the easy way in which Mr. Windibank—that is, my father—took it all. He would not go to the police, and he would not go to you, and so at last, as he would do nothing, and kept on saying that there was no harm done, it made me mad, and I just on with my things and came right away to you."

"Your father?" said Holmes. "Your stepfather, surely, since the name is different."

"Yes, my stepfather. I call him father, though it sounds funny, too, for he is only five years and two months older than myself."

"And your mother is alive?"

"Oh, yes; mother is alive and well. I wasn't best pleased, Mr. Holmes, when she married again so soon after father's death, and a man who was nearly fifteen years younger than herself. Father was a plumber in the Tottenham Court Road, and he left a tidy business behind him, which mother carried on with Mr. Hardy, the foreman; but when Mr. Windibank came he made her sell the business, for he was very superior, being a traveler in wines. They got four thousand seven hundred for the good-will and interest, which wasn't near as much as father could have got if he had been alive."

I had expected to see Sherlock Holmes impatient under this rambling and inconsequential narrative, but, on the contrary, he had listened with the greatest concentration of attention.

"Your own little income," he asked, "does it come out of the business?"

"Oh, no, sir. It is quite separate, and was left me by my Uncle Ned in Auckland. It is in New Zealand stock, paying four and half per cent. Two thousand five hundred pounds was the amount, but I can only touch the interest."

"You interest me extremely," said Holmes. "And since you draw so large a sum as a hundred a year, with what you earn into the bargain, you no doubt travel a little, and indulge yourself in every way. I believe that a single lady can get on very nicely upon an income of about sixty pounds."

"I could do with much less than that, Mr. Holmes, but you understand that as long as I live at home I don't wish to be a burden to them, and so they have the use of the money just while I am staying with them. Of course that is only just for the time. Mr. Windibank draws my interest every quarter, and pays it over to mother, and I find that I can do pretty well with what I earn at typewriting. It brings me twopence a sheet, and I can often do from fifteen to twenty sheets in a day."

"You have made your position very clear to me," said Holmes. "This is my friend, Doctor Watson, before whom you can speak as freely as before myself. Kindly tell us now all about your connection with Mr. Hosmer Angel."

A flush stole over Miss Sutherland's face, and she picked nervously at the fringe of her jacket. "I met him first at the gasfitters' ball," she said. "They used to send father tickets when he was alive, and then afterwards they remembered us, and sent them to mother. Mr. Windibank did not wish us to go. He never did wish us to go anywhere. He would get quite mad if I wanted so much as to join a Sunday School treat. But this time I was set on going, and I would go, for what right had he to prevent? He said the folk were not fit for us to know, when all father's friends were to be there. And he said that I had nothing fit to wear, when I had my purple plush that I had never so much as taken out of the drawer. At last, when nothing else would do, he went off to France upon the business of the firm; but we went, mother and I, with Mr. Hardy, who used to be our foreman, and it was there I met Mr. Hosmer Angel."

"I suppose," said Holmes, "that when Mr. Windibank came back from France, he was very annoyed at your having gone to the ball?"

"Oh, well, he was very good about it. He laughed, I remember, and shrugged his shoulders, and said there was no use denying anything to a woman, for she would have her way."

"I see. Then at the gasfitters' ball you met, as I understand, a gentleman called Mr. Hosmer Angel?"

"Yes, sir. I met him that night, and he called next day to ask if we had got home all safe, and after that we met him—that is to say, Mr. Holmes, I met him twice for walks, but after that father came back again, and Mr. Hosmer Angel could not come to the house any more."

"No?"

"Well, you know, father didn't like anything of the sort. He wouldn't have any visitors if he could help it, and he used to say that a woman should be happy in her own family circle. But then, as I used to say to mother, a woman wants her own circle to begin with, and I had not got mine yet."

"But how about Mr. Hosmer Angel? Did he make no attempt to see you?"

"Well, father was going off to France again in a week, and Hosmer wrote and said that it would be safer and better not to see each other until he had gone. We could write in the meantime, and he used to write every day. I took the letters in the morning, so there was no need for father to know."

"Were you engaged to the gentleman at this time?"

"Oh, yes, Mr. Holmes. We were engaged after the first walk that we took. Hosmer—Mr. Angel—was a cashier in an office in Leadenhall Street—and—"

"What office?"

"That's the worst of it, Mr. Holmes; I don't know."

"Where did he live, then?"

"He slept on the premises."

"And you don't know his address?"

"No—except that it was Leadenhall Street."

"Where did you address your letters, then?"

"To the Leadenhall Street Post Office, to be left till called for. He said that if they were sent to the office he would be chaffed by all the other clerks about having letters from a lady, so I offered to typewrite them, like he did his, but he wouldn't have that, for he said that when I wrote them they seemed to come from me, but when they were typewritten he always felt that the machine had come between us. That will just show you how fond he was of me, Mr. Holmes, and the little things that he would think of."

"It was most suggestive," said Holmes. "It has long been an axiom of mine that the little things are infinitely the most important.

Can you remember any other little things about Mr. Hosmer Angel?"

"He was a very shy man, Mr. Holmes. He would rather walk with me in the evening than in the daylight, for he said that he hated to be conspicuous. Very retiring and gentlemanly he was. Even his voice was gentle. He'd had the quinsy and swollen glands when he was young, he told me, and it had left him with a weak throat and a hesitating, whispering fashion of speech. He was always well dressed, very neat and plain, but his eyes were weak, just as mine are, and he wore tinted glasses against the glare."

"Well, and what happened when Mr. Windibank, your stepfather, returned to France?"

"Mr. Hosmer Angel came to the house again, and proposed that we should marry before father came back. He was in dreadful earnest, and made me swear, with my hands on the Testament, that whatever happened I would always be true to him. Mother said he was quite right to make me swear, and that it was a sign of his passion. Mother was all in his favor from the first, and was even fonder of him than I was. Then, when they talked of marrying within the week, I began to ask about father; but they both said never to mind about father, but just to tell him afterwards and mother said she would make it all right with him. I didn't quite like that, Mr. Holmes. It seemed funny that I should ask his leave, as he was only a few years older than me; but I didn't want to do anything on the sly, so I wrote to father at Bordeaux, where the company has its French offices, but the letter came back to me on the very morning of the wedding."

"It missed him, then?"

"Yes, sir, for he had started to England just before it arrived."

"Ha! that was unfortunate. Your wedding was arranged, then, for the Friday. Was it to be in church?"

"Yes, sir, but very quietly. It was to be at St. Saviour's, near King's Cross, and we were to have breakfast afterwards at the St. Pancras Hotel. Hosmer came for us in a hansom, but as there were two of us, he put us both into it, and stepped himself into a four-wheeler, which happened to be the only other cab in the street. We got to the church first, and when the four-wheeler drove up we waited for him to step out, but he never did, and when the cabman got down from the box and looked, there was no one there! The cabman said that he could not imagine what had become of him, for he had seen him get in with his own eyes. That was last Friday, Mr. Holmes, and I have never seen or heard anything since then to throw any light upon what became of him."

"It seems to me that you have been very shamefully treated," said Holmes.

"Oh, no, sir! He was too good and kind to leave me so. Why, all the morning he was saying to me that, whatever happened, I was to be true; and that even if something quite unforeseen occurred to separate us, I was always to remember that I was pledged to him, and that he would claim his pledge sooner or later. It seemed strange talk for a wedding morning, but what has happened since gives a meaning to it."

"Most certainly it does. Your own opinion is, then, that some unforeseen catastrophe has occurred to him?"

"Yes, sir. I believe that he foresaw some danger, or else he would not have talked so. And then I think that what he foresaw happened."

"But you have no notion as to what it could have been?"

"None."

"One more question. How did your mother take the matter?"

"She was angry, and said that I was never to speak of the matter again."

"And your father? Did you tell him?"

"Yes, and he seemed to think, with me, that something had happened, and that I should hear of Hosmer again. As he said, what interest could anyone have in bringing me to the door of the church, and then leaving me? Now, if he had borrowed my money, or if he had married me and got my money settled on him, there might be some reason; but Hosmer was very independent about money, and never would look at a shilling of mine. And yet what could have happened? And why could he not write? Oh! it drives me half mad to think of, and I can't sleep a wink at night." She pulled a little handkerchief out of her muff, and began to sob heavily into it.

"I shall glance into the case for you," said Holmes, rising, "and I have no doubt that we shall reach some definite result. Let the weight of the matter rest upon me now, and do not let your mind dwell upon it further. Above all, try to let Mr. Hosmer Angel vanish from your memory, as he has done from your life."

"Then you don't think I'll see him again?"

"I fear not."

"Then what has happened to him?"

"You will leave that question in my hands. I should like an accurate description of him, and any letters of his which you can spare."

"I advertised for him in last Saturday's *Chronicle*," said she. "Here is the slip, and here are four letters from him."

"Thank you. And your address?"

"No. 31 Lyon Place, Camberwell."

"Mr. Angel's address you never had, I understand. Where is your father's place of business?"

"He travels for Westhouse & Marbank, the great claret importers of Fenchurch Street."

"Thank you. You have made your statement very clearly. You will leave the papers here, and remember the advice which I have given you. Let the whole incident be a sealed book, and do not allow it to affect your life."

"You are very kind, Mr. Holmes, but I cannot do that. I shall be true to Hosmer. He shall find me ready when he comes back."

For all the preposterous hat and the vacuous face, there was something noble in the simple faith of our visitor which compelled our respect. She laid her little bundle of papers upon the table, and went her way, with a promise to come again whenever she might be summoned.

Sherlock Holmes sat silent for a few minutes with his finger tips still pressed together, his legs stretched out in front of him, and his gaze directed upward to the ceiling. Then he took down from the rack the old and oily clay pipe, which was to him as a counselor, and, having lighted it, he leaned back in his chair, with thick blue cloud wreaths spinning up from him, and a look of infinite languor in his face.

"Quite an interesting study, that maiden," he observed. "I found her more interesting than her little problem, which, by the way, is rather a trite one. You will find parallel cases, if you consult my index, in Andover in '77, and there was something of the sort at The Hague last year. Old as is the idea, however, there were one or two details which were new to me. But the maiden herself was most instructive."

"You appeared to read a good deal upon her which was quite invisible to me," I remarked.

"Not invisible, but unnoticed, Watson. You did not know where to look, and so you missed all that was important. I can never bring you to realize the importance of sleeves, the suggestiveness of thumb nails, or the great issues that may hang from a boot lace. Now, what did you gather from that woman's appearance? Describe it."

"Well, she had a slate-colored, broad-brimmed straw hat, with a feather of a brickish red. Her jacket was black, with black beads sewed upon it and a fringe of little black jet ornaments. Her dress was brown, rather darker than coffee color, with a little purple plush at the neck and sleeves. Her gloves were grayish, and were worn through at the right forefinger. Her boots I didn't observe. She had small round, hanging gold earrings, and a general air of being fairly well-to-do, in a vulgar, comfortable, easy-going way."

Sherlock Holmes clapped his hands softly together and chuckled.

"'Pon my word, Watson, you are coming along wonderfully. You have really done very well indeed. It is true that you have missed everything of importance, but you have hit upon the method, and you have a quick eye for color. Never trust to general impressions, my boy, but concentrate yourself upon details. My first glance is always at a woman's sleeve. In a man it is perhaps better first to take the knee of the trouser. As you observe, this woman had plush upon her sleeve, which is a most useful material for showing traces. The double line a little above the wrist, where the typewritist presses against the table, was beautifully defined. The sewing machine, of the hand type, leaves a similar mark, but only on the left arm, and on the side of it farthest from the thumb, instead of being right across the broadest part, as this was. I then glanced at her face, and observing the dint of a *pince-nez* at either side of her nose, I ventured a remark upon short sight and typewriting, which seemed to surprise her."

"It surprised me."

"But, surely, it was very obvious. I was then much surprised and interested on glancing down to observe that, though the boots which she was wearing were not unlike each other, they were really odd ones, the one having a slightly decorated toe cap and the other a plain one. One was buttoned only in the two lower buttons out of five, and the other at the first, third, and fifth. Now, when you see that a young lady, otherwise neatly dressed, has come away from home with odd boots, half-buttoned, it is no great deduction to say that she came away in a hurry."

"And what else?" I asked, keenly interested, as I always was, by my friend's incisive reasoning.

"I noted, in passing, that she had written a note before leaving home, but after being fully dressed. You observed that her right glove was torn at the forefinger, but you did not, apparently, see that both glove and finger were stained with violet ink. She had written in a hurry, and dipped her pen too deep. It must have been this morning, or the mark would not remain clear upon the finger. All this is amusing, though rather elementary, but I must go back to business, Watson. Would you mind reading me the advertised description of Mr. Hosmer Angel?"

I held the little printed slip to the light. "Missing," it said, "on the morning of the fourteenth, a gentleman named Hosmer Angel. About five feet seven inches in height; strongly built, sallow complexion, black hair, a little bald in the center, bushy black side-whiskers and mustache; tinted glasses; slight infirmity of speech. Was dressed, when last seen, in black frock-coat faced with silk, black waistcoat, gold Albert chain, and gray Harris tweed trousers, with brown gaiters over elastic-sided boots. Known to have been employed in an office in Leadenhall Street. Anybody bringing," etc., etc.

"That will do," said Holmes. "As to the letters," he continued, glancing over them, "they are very commonplace. Absolutely no clew in them to Mr. Angel, save that he quotes Balzac once. There is one remarkable point, however, which will no doubt strike you."

"They are typewritten," I remarked.

"Not only that, but the signature is typewritten. Look at the neat little 'Hosmer Angel' at the bottom. There is a date, you see, but no superscription except Leadenhall Street, which is rather vague. The point about the signature is very suggestive—in fact, we may call it conclusive."

"Of what?"

"My dear fellow, is it possible you do not see how strongly it bears upon the case?"

"I cannot say that I do, unless it were that he wished to be able to deny his signature if an action for breach of promise were instituted."

"No, that was not the point. However, I shall write two letters which should settle the matter. One is to a firm in the City, the other is to the young lady's stepfather, Mr. Windibank, asking him whether he could meet us here at six o'clock to-morrow evening. It is just as well that we should do business with the male relatives. And now, doctor, we can do nothing until the answers to those letters come, so we may put our little problem upon the shelf for the interim."

I had had so many reasons to believe in my friend's subtle powers of reasoning, and extraordinary energy in action, that I felt that he must have some solid grounds for the assured and easy demeanor with which he treated the singular mystery which he had been called upon to fathom. Once only had I known him to fail, in the case of the King of Bohemia and the Irene Adler photograph, but when I looked back to the weird business of the "Sign of the Four," and the extraordinary circumstances connected with the "Study in Scarlet," I felt that it would be a strange tangle indeed which he could not unravel.

I left him then, still puffing at his black clay pipe, with the conviction that when I came again on the next evening I would find that he held in his hands all the clews which would lead up to the identity of the disappearing bridegroom of Miss Mary Sutherland.

A professional case of great gravity was engaging my own attention at the time, and the whole of next day I was busy at the bedside of the sufferer. It was not until close upon six o'clock that I found myself free, and was able to spring into a hansom and drive to Baker Street, half afraid that I might be too late to assist at the *dénouement* of the little mystery. I found Sherlock Holmes alone, however, half asleep, with his long, thin form curled up in the recesses of his armchair. A formidable array of bottles and test-tubes, with the pungent, cleanly smell of hydrochloric acid, told me that he had spent his day in the chemical work which was so dear to him.

"Well, have you solved it?" I asked as I entered.

"Yes. It was the bisulphate of baryta."

"No, no; the mystery!" I cried.

"Oh, that! I thought of the salt that I have been working upon. There was never any mystery in the matter, though, as I said yesterday, some of the details are of interest. The only drawback is that there is no law, I fear, that can touch the scoundrel."

"Who was he, then, and what was his object in deserting Miss Sutherland?"

The question was hardly out of my mouth, and Holmes had not yet opened his lips to reply, when we heard a heavy footfall in the passage, and a tap at the door.

"This is the girl's stepfather, Mr. James Windibank," said Holmes. "He has written to me to say that he would be here at six. Come in!"

The man who entered was a sturdy, middle-sized fellow, some thirty years of age, clean shaven, and sallow-skinned, with a bland, insinuating manner, and a pair of wonderfully sharp and penetrating gray eyes. He shot a questioning glance at each of us, placed his shiny top hat upon the sideboard, and, with a slight bow, sidled down into the nearest chair.

"Good evening, Mr. James Windibank," said Holmes. "I think this typewritten letter is from you, in which you made an appointment with me for six o'clock?"

"Yes, sir. I am afraid that I am a little late, but I am not quite my own master, you know. I am sorry that Miss Sutherland has troubled you about this little matter, for I think it is far better not to wash linen of the sort in public. It was quite against my wishes that she came, but she is a very excitable, impulsive girl, as you may have noticed, and she is not easily controlled when she has made up her mind on a point. Of course, I did not mind you so much, as you are not connected with the official police, but it is not pleasant to have a family misfortune like this noised abroad. Besides, it is a useless expense, for how could you possibly find this Hosmer Angel?"

"On the contrary," said Holmes, quietly, "I have every reason to believe that I will succeed in discovering Mr. Hosmer Angel."

Mr. Windibank gave a violent start, and dropped his gloves. "I am delighted to hear it," he said.

"It is a curious thing," remarked Holmes, "that a typewriter has really quite as much individuality as a man's handwriting. Unless they are quite new no two of them write exactly alike. Some letters get more worn than others, and some wear only on one side. Now, you remark in this note of yours, Mr. Windibank, that in every case there is some little slurring over the *e*, and a slight defect in the tail of the *r*. There are fourteen other characteristics, but those are the more obvious."

"We do all our correspondence with this machine at the office, and no doubt it is a little worn," our visitor answered, glancing keenly at Holmes with his bright little eyes.

"And now I will show you what is really a very interesting study, Mr. Windibank," Holmes continued. "I think of writing another little monograph some of these days on the typewriter and its relation to crime. It is a subject to which I have devoted some little attention. I have here four letters which purport to come from the missing man. They are all typewritten. In each case, not only are the *e*'s slurred and the *r*'s tailless, but you will observe, if you care to use my magnifying lens, that the fourteen other characteristics to which I have alluded are there as well."

Mr. Windibank sprung out of his chair, and picked up his hat. "I cannot waste time over this sort of fantastic talk, Mr. Holmes," he said. "If you can catch the man, catch him, and let me know when you have done it."

"Certainly," said Holmes, stepping over and turning the key in the door. "I let you know, then, that I have caught him!"

"What! where?" shouted Mr. Windibank, turning white to his lips, and glancing about him like a rat in a trap.

"Oh, it won't do—really it won't," said Holmes, suavely. "There is no possible getting out of it, Mr. Windibank. It is quite too transparent, and it was a very bad compliment when you said that it was impossible for me to solve so simple a question. That's right! Sit down, and let us talk it over."

Our visitor collapsed into a chair, with a ghastly face, and a glitter of moisture on his brow. "It—it's not actionable," he stammered.

"I am very much afraid that it is not; but between ourselves, Windibank, it was as cruel, and selfish, and heartless a trick in a petty way as ever came before me. Now, let me just run over the course of events, and you will contradict me if I go wrong."

The man sat huddled up in his chair, with his head sunk upon his breast, like one who is utterly crushed. Holmes stuck his feet up on the corner of the mantelpiece, and, leaning back with his hands in his pockets, began talking, rather to himself, as it seemed, than to us.

"The man married a woman very much older than himself for her money," said he, "and he enjoyed the use of the money of the daughter as long as she lived with them. It was a considerable sum, for people in their position, and the loss of it would have made a serious difference. It was worth an effort to preserve it. The daughter was of a good, amiable disposition, but affectionate and warm-hearted in her ways, so that it was evident that with her fair personal advantages, and her little income, she would not be allowed to remain single long. Now her marriage would mean, of course, the loss of a hundred a year, so what does her stepfather do to prevent it? He takes the obvious course of keeping her at home, and forbidding her to seek the company of people of her own age. But soon he found that that would not answer forever. She became restive, insisted upon her rights, and finally announced her positive intention of going to a certain ball. What does her clever stepfather do then? He conceives an idea more creditable to his head than to his heart. With the connivance and assistance of his wife, he disguised himself, covered those keen eyes with tinted glasses masked the face with a mustache and a pair of bushy whiskers, sunk that clear voice into an insinuating whisper, and doubly secure on account of the girl's short sight, he appears as Mr. Hosmer Angel, and keeps off other lovers by making love himself."

"It was only a joke at first," groaned our visitor. "We never thought that she would have been so carried away."

"Very likely not. However that may be, the young lady was very decidedly carried away, and having quite made up her mind that her stepfather was in France, the suspicion of treachery never for an instant entered her mind. She was flattered by the gentleman's attentions, and the effect was increased by the loudly expressed admiration of her mother. Then Mr. Angel began to call, for it was obvious that the matter should be pushed as far as if would go, if a real effect were to be produced. There were meetings, and an engagement, which would finally secure the girl's affections from turning toward anyone else. But the deception could not be kept up forever. These pretended journeys to France were rather cumbrous. The thing to do was clearly to bring the business to an end in such a dramatic manner that it would leave a permanent impression upon the young lady's mind, and prevent her from looking upon any other suitor for some time to come. Hence those vows of fidelity exacted upon a Testament, and hence also the allusions to a possibility of something happening on the very morning of the wedding. James Windibank wished Miss Sutherland to be so bound to Hosmer Angel, and so uncertain as to his fate, that for ten years to come, at any rate, she would not listen to another man. As far as the church door he brought her, and then, as he could go no farther, he conveniently vanished away by the old trick of stepping in at one door of a four-wheeler and out at the other. I think that that was the chain of events, Mr. Windibank!"

Our visitor had recovered something of his assurance while Holmes had been talking, and he rose from his chair now with a cold sneer upon his pale face.

"It may be so, or it may not, Mr. Holmes," said he; "but if you are so very sharp you ought to be sharp enough to know that it is you who are breaking the law now, and not me. I have done nothing actionable from the first, but as long as you keep that door locked you lay yourself open to an action for assault and illegal constraint."

"The law cannot, as you say, touch you," said Holmes, unlocking and throwing open the door, "yet there never was a man who deserved punishment more. If the young lady has a brother or a friend, he ought to lay a whip across your shoulders. By Jove!" he continued, flushing up at the sight of the bitter sneer upon the man's face, "it is not part of my duties to my client, but here's a hunting crop handy, and I think I shall just treat myself to—" He took two swift steps to the whip, but before he could grasp it there was a wild clatter of steps upon the stairs, the heavy hall door banged, and from the window we could see Mr. James Windibank running at the top of his speed down the road.

"There's a cold-blooded scoundrel!" said Holmes, laughing as he threw himself down into his chair once more. "That fellow will rise from crime to crime until he does something very bad and ends on a gallows. The case has, in some respects, been not entirely devoid of interest."

"I cannot now entirely see all the steps of your reasoning," I remarked.

"Well, of course it was obvious from the first that this Mr. Hosmer Angel must have some strong object for his curious conduct, and it was equally clear that the only man who really profited by the incident, as far as we could see, was the stepfather. Then the fact that the two men were never together, but that the one always appeared when the other was away, was suggestive. So were the tinted spectacles and the curious voice, which both hinted at a disguise, as did the bushy whiskers. My suspicions were all confirmed by his peculiar action in typewriting his signature, which, of course, inferred that his handwriting was so familiar to her that she would recognize even the smallest sample of it. You see all these isolated facts, together with many minor ones, all pointed in the same direction."

"And how did you verify them?"

"Having once spotted my man, it was easy to get corroboration. I knew the firm for which this man worked. Having taken the printed description, I eliminated everything from it which could be the result of a disguise,—the whiskers, the glasses, the voice – and I sent it to the firm with a request that they would inform me whether it answered to the description of any of their travelers. I had already noticed the peculiarities of the typewriter, and I wrote to the man himself at his business address, asking him if he would come here. As I expected, his reply was typewritten, and revealed the same trivial but characteristic defects. The same post brought me a letter from Westhouse & Marbank, of Fenchurch Street, to say that the description tallied in every respect with that of their employee, James Windibank. *Voilá tout!*"

"And Miss Sutherland?"

"If I tell her she will not believe me. You may remember the old Persian saying, 'There is danger for him who taketh the tiger cub, and danger also for whoso snatcheth a delusion from a woman.' There is as much sense in Hafiz as in Horace, and as much knowledge of the world."

✗